A BOY FROM THE BLUE

Her fiancé would be outraged. But how could Annabelle abandon the little boy who had been left in the cabin of her ship. There was no way to return him, as she hadn't the slightest idea where he belonged. And, mysteriously, his luggage bore her address . . .

Surely someone would claim him when they reached shore! If they didn't—there was only one person to whom she could turn for help—handsome, charming, **maddening** Angus Pemberton, the one man on earth she thoroughly detested . . .

THE FOX FROM HIS LAIR

ELIZABETH CADELL
THE FOX
FROM HIS LAIR

A NATIONAL GENERAL COMPANY

Ⓦ

THE FOX FROM HIS LAIR

*A Bantam Book / published by arrangement with
William Morrow & Co., Inc.*

PRINTING HISTORY

William Morrow edition published January 1966
2nd printing.......January 1966
3rd printing..........April 1966
Serialized in THE CHICAGO TRIBUNE *under the title*
Why Did He Come Back?
Bantam edition published August 1970
2nd printing

*Bantam Books are published by Bantam Books, Inc., a National
General company. Its trade-mark, consisting of the words "Bantam
Books" and the portrayal of a bantam, is registered in the United
States Patent Office and in other countries. Marca Registrada.
Bantam Books, Inc., 666 Fifth Avenue, New York, N.Y. 10019.*

PRINTED IN THE UNITED STATES OF AMERICA

Chapter One

SOMEBODY ONCE WROTE something, Anabelle Baird reflected, about every prospect pleasing and only man being vile. Shakespeare, probably . . . but no; come to think of it, prospect pleases had rhymed with spicy breezes. A hymn.

Hymn or Shakespeare, the sentiment summed up her visit to Lisbon. She had seen little but the city and its environs, but she had found the prospects more than pleasing. Vile was the term that could most fittingly have been applied to her host and hostess.

She found nothing wrong with the prospect at the airport at this moment. Her senses, sun-warmed, drank in the brilliant light, the gentle breeze, the line of low, distant hills. Seated on the balcony of the airport buildings, she looked out over a wide, peaceful plain edged by little rust-roofed houses, with steel-blue skies above and a dark blue sea not far away.

She felt very happy. On her arrival two weeks ago, she had experienced a similar sense of elation, caused by the knowledge that she was going to see her fiancé. She had to admit that her present pleasure sprang largely from the thought of leaving him.

She reviewed the past two weeks with a mind that struggled for detachment. Philip had perhaps had cause for anger; he didn't like any little boys at any time, and he had seen no reason why John and James should not have been left in England. It wasn't, he had argued in four telegrams and a heated telephone call before she left home, it wasn't as though they were his children or her children. Why, he had demanded angrily on her arrival, had she blown his whole plan to pieces, ruined the visit he had so carefully arranged, foisted her sister's children on entire strangers; in short, why had she destroyed the prime purpose of the trip, designed to show his employers the charming girl he was shortly to marry. Why? He would tell her why: to oblige yet again a sister who went through life assuming that she could at any time, and without notice, pack up and go off with her husband while somebody else—somebody else? who else but Anabelle?—took over the boys. And what boys! Savages, if ever he saw savages. To bring them out, uninvited, to let them loose in a house full—hadn't he told her how full?—of beautiful things, most of them fragile; to cloud the pleasant relations he had so carefully built up with his Chief and his Chief's wife . . .

Et cetera.

Rescuing the two glasses and the innumerable battered straws through which her two small nephews had sucked highly coloured orangeade, she summoned a waiter, paid the bill, and led the boys downstairs and into the open to work off some of their supercharged spirits before imprisoning them in the plane that was to convey them to Oporto. They ran ahead, stumbling and shouting, to a railing up which they could scramble in order to view the three planes standing on the tarmac.

"*That* one," said James, aged five and already noted for his superior intelligence, "that one is the one that we're going on."

"Going *in*," corrected his four-year-old brother. "You can't go *on* a naeroplane; you go *in* one. Don't you, Aunt Anabelle?"

She nodded and with a handkerchief endeavoured to remove orangeade stains from his diminutive trousers. The two small faces were upturned to hers, and as she looked down at them a feeling of pride coursed suddenly through her. They were nice children, she thought. Red-haired, like their mother; with little round noses, faintly freckled, and blue eyes filled with confidence in the pleasantness and security of life. It was a confidence which she had done more than anybody to engender. Clare loved them, but Clare was more wife than mother, and the choice between staying with the boys or accompanying their father was easily made. Clare had gone, but Anabelle had always been there. . . .

"Where's Philip gone?" James asked.

"You know quite well where he's gone," Anabelle said. "He had to go chasing after Mr. and Mrs. Jansen because you took her brooch."

"I didn't *take* it," he explained patiently. "I *told* you, Aunt Anabelle. It came off her dress and I picked it up and I was holding it to tell her, but I forgot because she didn't stop talking. She talked and talked."

True enough, Anabelle acknowledged to herself. Two weeks of that voice, harsh and unceasing and Swedish-English. "No, no, Anabelle, the boys must stay away from this room because here is my priceless china." "No, Anabelle; I am sorry, but I cannot ask my cook for special food for the children; I did not, as you know, expect to have children visiting with me."

She had disliked the children, and the children had disliked her. Philip had spent his time shooing them out of Mrs. Jansen's sight. The boys had not liked him before; they now liked him even less. Two happy weeks . . .

She shook off her preoccupation and instigated a game of catch-me that worked off the boys' energy without giving her more than mild exercise in evasive tactics. She remembered with gratitude that they were leaving Lisbon, leaving Philip, leaving his Chief —why did Philip always insist on calling him his Chief?—leaving his crow-voiced wife. They were going to Oporto, where Clare and her husband Keith awaited them. They were going on to stay with the Prendergasts, port producers, in their beautiful, rambling Quinta on the slopes of the Douro, where the boys would be welcomed and absorbed into the hordes of little boys and girls who lived on the estate. There was space and comfort at the Prendergasts', and no priceless china; Mr. Prendergast and his brother George had very loud voices, but they rang with good will; Dinah and Margaret bounced and shrieked, but they had insisted on having the children as well as Anabelle and Clare and Keith.

There were few people at the airport. Two or three tables in the restaurant had been occupied by late lunchers. On the balcony a few people sat sipping cool drinks; here, on the ground, a sprinkling of spectators gazed at the stationary planes. The other passengers for the Oporto flight were assembled in the departure lounge, sheltered from the late May sunshine. Only Annabelle and the two small boys were active.

Circling to avoid them as they rushed past her, laughing as they missed her, she became aware of a man leaning negligently over the railing of the balcony and looking down at them. Her gaze swept past him; her attention scarcely left the boys, now employing a more wary approach—and then something drew her eyes back to the leaning figure and a flood of memories—all unwelcome—filled her mind.

It couldn't be. He was thousands of miles away, and everybody had said, with conviction, that he would never come back. It was a resemblance, that was all; this was Portugal, and on every side were men with dark hair and dark eyes and . . .

But there was no mistaking that expression: a mixture of the bland and the sardonic. There was no mistaking that lean figure or even that too-familiar attitude. It couldn't, it couldn't be. . . .

She ventured one more glance. It was.

The airport, the laughing, breathless boys, the scattered figures on the tarmac and behind the railing, all disappeared. For moments, she was back in the garden of her home, shouting with hatred at the enemy leaning negligently over the wall—the enemy who had ruined every holiday and every outdoor project, who had throughout the long years of her childhood defeated, effortlessly, every attempt at revenge.

Angus Pemberton.

The past receded. She was back in the Lisbon sunshine, playing with her two nephews. She could only hope that Angus Pemberton was not on his way home —but it was hardly possible, she remembered with relief; he had been thrown out by his grandmother, who had stated positively that he had gone for good —for everybody's good.

There was a hope that he had not recognized her. It was, she calculated, seven years since he had left Steyne. She had been eighteen, and although she could not have changed in essentials, fashions made an effective disguise; he might trace a likeness, but that would be all.

The hope weakened when she saw, without seeming to see, that he had left the balcony. It revived for a moment as he hesitated outside the airport buildings —and died when he began a leisurely, long-legged, purposeful approach.

There was no chance of moving away, even if she had wanted to; the boys had caught her during her moment off-guard, and she was encircled by their arms. She glanced at her watch: twenty minutes before the plane was due to leave; Mrs. Jansen, anxious to avoid a last luncheon, had stated that they must be at the airport in good time—and so they had been.

She could hear, behind her, the firm footsteps. Then the slow, deep voice—that, too, she remembered well.

"Aren't you . . . surely you're Anabelle Baird?"

She turned. She managed a smile, but her greeting was cool.

"Hello, Angus. What are you doing here?"

"Waiting for a hired car. I ordered one, but it wasn't here when I flew in. It's on its way. And you?"

"I'm going up to Oporto."

"You married"—his eyes went to the boys—"a Portuguese?"

"These are Clare's children."

He smiled. Well might he smile, she reflected bitterly; it had taken him ten minutes and a lift of the eyebrows to transform Clare's lifelong enmity into a river of devotion that had almost, but unfortunately not quite, drowned him.

He was screwing up his eyes in calculation.

"Clare was, let me see, seventeen when I left. And pretty. Did she marry that concert pianist?"

"No."

"The architect—what was his name?"

"No."

"The fellow with the woolly hair, who called me a low swine?"

"No. She married Keith Trevor, a journalist."

"Lucky journalist. What are you doing with her children?"

"I'm looking after them."

"And doing it remarkably well."

There it was—that sardonic note she knew so well.

"Didn't you marry anybody?" he asked.

He hadn't, she noticed—and it did not increase her regard for him—made any pretense of listing the candidates. She had to face it; she had, in fact, faced it long ago: she wasn't the type that made men catch fire.

"No, I didn't marry anybody," she said.

There was a pause while he studied her frankly—to assess, she thought, exactly where she had missed out. She felt the colour rising to her cheeks, but she met his gaze steadily.

He saw a small, slight girl—not more than five feet two, he judged. A delicate, oval faced framed by curtains of straight, soft hair so fair as to look almost silvery. Eyes brown, their expression the half-watchful, half-suspicious one he remembered. She had a very direct gaze. A soft, curved mouth; small nose, perfect skin. By any standards attractive; perhaps too cool, too sane, too sensible to be termed seductive.

"Where's Clare now?" he asked.

"Her husband travels around a lot. Where he goes, Clare goes."

"And leaves the children with you?"

"Why not? I enjoy having them."

"Is she based in Portugal?"

"No. She and Keith rent a cottage on Mrs. Morton's grounds."

"Mrs. Morton?" He laughed—the sudden, deep, and, she had to admit, infectious laugh she remembered. She herself had never caught the infection. "I remember. Two, or was it three divorced husbands who kept reappearing? I rather liked her; she used to make Steyne stir in its sleep, which was quite a feat. She had a son I couldn't stand—can't recall his name —Ancell. Yes, Philip Ancell. What happened to him; is he still around?"

"Yes, he is. I'm going to marry him."

"No!" Not, she noted indignantly, not a second's embarrassment. Certainly he hadn't changed. "We can't be talking about the same fellow, because I distinctly remember your calling him a . . . well, not before the children. He could have grown out of his boyish imperfections, but you really ought to reconsider; he was always given to whining."

Was, and is, she would have liked to reply, with the memory of the last two weeks coming back to her mind.

"You haven't seen him for seven years," she said instead. "The time you saw him, you tried to drown him."

"Nonsense. I was only holding his head under water until he said he was sorry for tripping me up."

His mind had gone back to the picture he had seen from the balcony; playing with the children, she had shown a gentleness and tenderness he had never seen in her; she had looked the very symbol of motherhood: devoted, protective, patient. Undoubtedly Ancell had reacted to the maternal touch. It was a pity; a man like that could never manage a girl like this—and a girl like this needed managing.

"Speaking of home," he said, "how is my grandmother?"

"Why didn't you ever write and ask her?"

"When she requested me to leave, she intimated that correspondence wouldn't be welcomed. I've had, of course, my secret sources of information."

She could guess some of them. There were several

women who would have liked to keep in touch, or keep him in touch—if he had been so careless as to leave an address.

"Then you know I've been working for your grandmother for the last five years," she said.

"Yes. Do you have to parade in the forecourt and march smartly to your desk?"

"No."

"No lining up for inspection?"

"None."

"She must have changed a good deal. All those military trophies still hanging in the hall?"

"Yes. You know quite well they're still hanging up. You know as well as I do that she'll never take them down."

"Does she still hold those reunions?"

She hesitated.

"There's not much response these days," she admitted. "Most of them send excuses, and those who do come—"

"I know. Come purely in a spirit of curiosity. Horses sold, I suppose?"

"Yes."

"Who looks after the grounds?"

"Your grandmother planted a lot of trees—there's much less garden and much more wood. A firm in Steyne sends out gardeners on a contract basis, and they keep the place more or less in hand."

"Foreign maids still?"

"No. Two widows; they've furnished some rooms in what used to be the servants' wing, and they've settled down and everything goes very well—they work from nine to five, in shifts or together, just as they please, and they're there all night, which is a good thing."

"It sounds more peaceful than it used to be. Who does my grandmother find to drill nowadays?"

"She doesn't drill anybody. I thought it was time she . . . well, thought about something else, so I suggested her doing what she's doing now."

"Sort of shop, isn't it?"

"Yes. She turned two of the ground-floor rooms

into a place where people could bring anything they
wanted to sell—she sells on a percentage basis, or they
give the things outright; all the proceeds go to charity. She enjoys it, and it keeps her busy; she does
most of the selling."

"And what do you do?"

"The paper work. I also keep an eye on her housekeeping, which doesn't interest her much nowadays."

"I hope the old martial spirit doesn't revive when
she sees me again," he said.

"You're . . . you're going home?" she asked in surprise.

He looked down at her, his lips widening in a smile.

"Where else?"

She found herself stammering.

"I thought . . . I imagined that when you left . . .
Certainly your grandmother said nothing about expecting you."

"I wrote to her; perhaps you left England before
she got the letter. Did you think I'd left Steyne for
ever?"

"Everybody thought you'd left Steyne for ever."

"I admit I thought so myself. But I've served seven
years, like that chap in the Bible. Now I'm older, and
Granny's older, and we've had time to simmer down.
So I'm going home—perhaps for good." He frowned
thoughtfully. "You had a schoolgirl sister—Olivia.
Where's Olivia?"

"In London."

"Working?"

"Not yet. Studying commercial art."

"Nice child, she was. She didn't have a quick temper, like you, and she had more in her head than
Clare. Be interesting to see her again."

How interesting, he had yet to learn, mused Anabelle. When he left Steyne, Olivia had been a thin,
painfully plain, totally unpromising eleven, absorbed
in the struggle to get into the junior netball team.
There had been no hint, in face or figure, of what she
was to become. If she told him that Olivia was . . .
Well, let him wait and see.

"She'll be home for two weeks in June," she said.

He had the boys' wrists imprisoned, a pair in each of his hands, and was swinging them effortlessly round in circles.

"More," demanded James when he allowed their feet to touch the ground.

"Presently. I want to talk to your aunt. Go and see if you can climb onto that fire engine over there."

They were away before Anabelle could frame a protest.

"And now," Angus said, "we can talk. Why didn't your fiancé come to Portugal with you?"

"He's here already. I came out to stay with his Ch— the man he works for, and his wife, Mr. and Mrs. Jansen. Jansen's Paper Mills. Philip opened up the offices in Paris and Milan, and now he's doing the same in Lisbon. I brought Clare's children because I promised Clare I'd look after them."

"Couldn't you have left them with your father?"

"No, I couldn't. Once he gets down to work, he forgets everything else."

"With Olivia?"

"Olivia lives in a fourth-floor flat with a balcony, and the boys would have been alone all day."

His dark eyes held hers for a moment in a casual survey.

"And you didn't leave home and go up to London. You stayed at home and fell in love with Ancell?"

"Yes."

He studied the boys, who, having failed to board the fire engine, were on their way back.

"Where's Ancell now?" he asked. "If he doesn't hurry, he'll miss the plane."

"He's not traveling. I'm going to meet Clare and her husband, and we're going to stay with the Prendergasts."

"Prendergasts . . . Yes, I remember. Two girls who stayed with you once."

"You ought to remember," she said coldly. "You cut the ropes of our tent, sank our canoe, put moles into our sleeping bags, played a hose onto our hammocks, and let the bull out while we were picnicking.

Looking back, I've often wondered if you weren't suffering from arrested development."

"Could be," he admitted readily. His eyes swept over her. "You haven't changed."

As so often in the past, she was left to draw her own conclusions as to what he intended to convey; now, as then, she had a strong suspicion that he had conveyed anything but a compliment.

She saw Philip's tall form in the distance, and Angus, following her glance, turned and watched him as he approached. Philip's expression, already clouded, underwent a variety of changes as he scanned the figure of the man standing beside Anabelle; incredulity was followed by a dismayed recognition which gave way, as he joined them, to a look that contained nothing of cordiality.

"Hello, Pemberton. Just in, or just off?"

"Oh in, in," Angus said in reassuring tones. "I couldn't believe it was Anabelle when I looked down from the top storey. By the way, congratulations."

"Thanks."

"When are you to be married?" he asked them.

"End of July," Philip said shortly. "Look, Anabelle, it's time—"

"End of July? A garden wedding, I hope," Angus said.

"If you're on the other side of the wall, no," said Philip. "Anabelle had too many of your neighbourly attentions before you left for Brazil."

"So she's just been telling me. Pity I didn't know she was going to be here; I'm driving up to Oporto, and I could have given her a lift."

"Thanks." Philip contrived to give the word the minimum of warmth. "Well, we've got to go. Good-bye."

"For the present," Angus amended pleasantly.

Anabelle turned to await the boys and found them ranging themselves on either side of Angus; as she walked ahead with Philip, she could hear him teaching them the names of the three types of aircraft on the ground; glancing back, she saw them some distance behind, with Angus effortlessly defeating an attempt on James's part to board a passing luggage truck.

"Why couldn't he have stayed in Brazil?" Philip demanded. "The town's been relatively peaceful for the past seven years. Did he say he'd made it up with his grandmother?"

"No."

"Well, I'll tell you one thing: if I can keep him out, he won't be at our wedding."

She glanced at his sullen expression.

"Grow up," she advised. "He was a nuisance when we were children, but we've moved forward a few stages—I hope."

"It's all very well for you to take that let-bygones-be-bygones attitude," he said resentfully. "All he did was annoy you. He didn't make you look a fool. He didn't knock you down on the slightest provocation when you were young, and he didn't spoil your chances with every girl you tried to make up to when you were older. All you've got to forgive is irritations, but in my case it's—"

"Nobody asked you to forgive; all you're required to do is forget. Was Mrs. Jansen glad to have her brooch back?"

"If she was, she didn't say so. To be absolutely frank, they were both—she and the Chief—pretty straight about how they felt about your visit."

She took a deep breath and did her best to choke down the resentment that had been accumulating since her arrival in Lisbon, but she could not forget the petty persecution to which Mrs. Jansen had subjected her, and which Philip had done nothing to stem. His attitude had throughout been one of peevishness towards herself and—in her view—undue deference towards his employers. Rage came suddenly to the surface and boiled over.

"To go on being absolutely frank," she said, "I didn't care for my visit either. I didn't want to come in the first place, as I told you; there was an air of being on show that I didn't appreciate. I also told you

quite clearly that I couldn't come without the boys.
Mrs. Jansen had a large house and more servants than
I could count; it wouldn't have hurt her to detach one
of them to keep an eye on John and James—instead
of which you all decided to make it two weeks of
penance for me just because I did what I thought was
right instead of what you and that cow of a Mrs. Jansen thought was right. If you'd let me go straight to
Oporto, as I suggested, everything would have worked
out: I'd have handed the boys over to Clare and Keith,
you would have come up to the Prendergasts' for a
long week-end—and you would have come in a good
mood."

"The whole trouble was that you didn't care, never
have cared, about making a good impression on the
Jansens."

"And never will care. What's so special about the
Jansens? He's a bully and she's a selfish, spoilt, overfed
. . . I nearly said sow."

"They employ me."

"So would anybody else. You're efficient, aren't
you? You've expanded their business, haven't you?
They owe you a good deal more than your salary,
and you could make them sit up and beg instead of
sitting up and begging yourself. Instead of which
you've allowed them to spend the last two weeks looking down their noses at me, and you've stood by
doing nothing while they've treated the boys like little
lepers. Anybody but the Jansens would have enjoyed
having two nice little boys like—"

"Are we going to be landed with your nieces and
nephews all our lives?"

"I haven't got any nieces—yet. One of these days
we might want to leave our children with Clare—and
when we do, Keith will enjoy having them, and he'll
be happy with them, just as I am with his. I *like* small
boys—*any* small boys—a whole lot better than I like
grownups like your Jansens."

"Well, don't shout; somebody might know them."

"Then they'd agree with everything I've said. And
if you're coming up to the Prendergasts' looking as

disagreeable as you've looked since I arrived, you'd better stay down here. If I hadn't been so busy with the boys, I would have—"

She stopped abruptly. Half-turning to drive home her point, she had become aware that Angus Pemberton, with the boys, was almost on their heels. The boys, intent on watching an incoming jet, had been silent; Angus Pemberton had also been silent—simply, she decided with hopeless anger filling her, to listen to what she was saying. How much he had heard she could only conjecture, but the expression on his face —a purposely blank, gazing-into-the-distance look— told her that he had heard a good deal and had enjoyed every word.

She had told Philip that they were grown up, but at this moment she did not feel it; she was filled with a longing to scratch Angus Pemberton's politely blank face. With an effort at self-control, she turned to him, said a brief word of farewell, and shepherded the two boys towards the departure lounge.

Once they were aboard the plane, her relief at leaving Philip predominated over all other emotions—but as the journey progressed, he was forgotten in the excitement of looking forward to the meeting with Clare and Keith. Instead of reproaches, there would soon be laughter; instead of the Jansens' grudging hospitality, there would be the Prendergasts in their sprawling Quinta on the slopes of the Douro, waiting with a warm welcome.

It was not her first visit; she and Clare had come out while they were at school with Dinah and Margaret Prendergast, and had stayed throughout the picturesque ceremonies attending the *vindima*, or grape harvest. Keith, born in Oporto, had known the Prendergasts all his life; it was their letter of introduction he had carried to London and presented to Clare, so that they had good reason to claim that they had made the match.

The plane touched down smoothly and soon the waiting figures became clear enough to distinguish— and as always when she saw Clare after even a brief interval, Anabelle was moved by her beauty. Not as lovely as Olivia, but lovely in a different and perhaps a warmer way. She had, however, none of Olivia's up-to-the-minute elegance; totally uninterested in clothes, she put on the first thing that came to hand and went out in it to enjoy life.

Beside her, her husband looked as ugly as ever. He was square and short and stocky, with untidy, hay-coloured hair; his chin stuck out aggressively, his eyes were too small and his nose too big. His air was deceptively lazy. At thirty-two a successful journalist, he was also a successful husband and father; sensing his merit, Anabelle had hoped but had scarcely expected that Clare would marry him; Clare herself said that she did so in an attempt to redress the balance of Nature.

It was wonderful to be with them again. Telling them so, she could think of nothing better by way of explanation than that they were a refreshing oasis after a desert of Jansen.

"Bad as that, was it?" Keith asked.

"It was terrible. One more week and I would have pushed Philip into the Tagus."

"Pity," Keith said, and she knew that he meant that it was a pity that she had not stayed one more week. You might call Philip a lot of things, she mused, but you couldn't call him popular.

They settled themselves in Keith's car and took the road to Amarante; Keith drove with one of the boys asleep against him; behind, the other slept on Clare's knee, and she and Anabelle fell into the easy exchange that passed for conversation.

"Were the boys good?"

"Considering the treatment they got, they were angels. She was a mean woman; she gave me no chance to keep them amused. In the end, I used to take them out morning and evening for exercise and stay out as long as I could."

"I told you Philip would be annoyed; you know he isn't keen on children."

"He'll get over it. How did your trip go?"

"We didn't go to Spain. Halfway there, Keith got a wire asking him to do an article on the port country, so that's what he's been doing."

"Then you haven't seen the Prendergasts?"

"No. Didn't get as far as that. We stuck around the schist country. Ever heard of schist?"

"Never."

"Neither had I. I'm still not sure what it is, but—"

"Crystalline rocks with a foliated structure," came from Keith.

"So now you know," Clare said. "Simple, really. I've got the whole thing taped. If you want good port, you've got to have schist, because the right port grapes will grow only on this schist; so it follows that where the schist is, there the good port is, because if you don't have schist, you can't grow special grapes and therefore you can't make special port. Clear?"

"As crystalline rocks."

"If you want any other little details, just ask. Any news from home?"

"Short letter from Father; he said Olivia's going to be home for two weeks in June."

"With a man, naturally. Which one this time?"

"Fellow student."

"One thing about Olivia's entourage," observed Keith, "is that they're not drones, any one of them. But young." He sighed. "The last one looked like my son."

"Which reminds me," Clare said. "I'm going to have another one, Anabelle."

"Clare! Are you absolutely sure? When?"

"November," Keith said. "She says son because she thinks that if she says son and touches wood, it'll turn out to be what she wants—a daughter."

"And when he arrives," Clare said, "we're going to look for a house of our own."

"In fact, we're not going to wait until he arrives," said Keith. "Small house and a big garden. Then you can get married and hand over your children to us for a change."

"Where are you going to have this small house and big garden?"

"In or around London—where else?" asked Clare.

"And where are you going to have the baby?"

"At home, if you and Father can bear it."

"You're going to bear it. It looks like being a crowded summer. I ran into Angus Pemberton on Lisbon airport."

While Clare was too astonished to do more than emit a long "We-e-ll!" Keith was putting himself into the picture.

"That's the chap next door?"

Nobody answered the question; Anabelle and Clare were both back in the past. Angus Pemberton's favourite spot—in justice they had had to admit that it was also his refuge—had been just the other side of the wall that divided his grandmother's thirty-acre grounds from their father's half-acre of garden. A screened, sloping patch by the wall had been the only place in which he could be certain of being out of sight of the windows of the house; at the foot of the slope he had made himself a small rush shelter, and from there he could have warning of his grandmother's approach—and from there launch attacks on Anabelle and Clare and in a lesser degree, for Olivia had been so much younger, on the three of them. They had been hopelessly handicapped, for while he had only to walk up the slope on his side to overlook their activities, their side was level, and against the wall grew a short, thick holly hedge impossible to penetrate. They had rigged tents, slowly and laboriously; they had fixed hammocks; they had spread picnics—for this was their only stretch of lawn and the sunniest part of their garden. He had only to lean over, and tents had sagged, hammocks had thumped to the ground, and crawling creatures had been deposited, from the end of a long pole, onto ham sandwiches or jam rolls. Later, his proximity had ruined any opportunities for romantic sessions on warm, moonlit nights, since these were liable to be shattered at any moment by a cough—or worse still, a laugh—from the other side of the wall.

Clare came out of her reverie and spoke reminiscently.

"Funny; I loathed him just as much as Anabelle did —until my seventeenth birthday."

"Ha. And then?" enquired Keith.

"Then he met me going along the path in the woods, and when I told him it was my birthday he kissed me. Wow!"

"Proceed," invited Keith.

"Well, as his lips touched mine, I felt everything slipping—my past, my failure to recognize a real man when I saw one, my up-till-then conviction that kissing wasn't all it was advertised to be, my feeling that love was a pretty tame amusement, my—"

"His lips must have touched yours for quite a time," Keith commented.

"It was what the books call a timeless moment. From then on—"

"—you joined the queue," ended Anabelle.

"I was the head of the queue; he kept telling me so. And then just as I was reading up on how to hook these elusive types, he had this terrible row with his grandmother and disappeared into the Brazilian jungle."

"What was this terrible row about?"

"The place got too small to hold him, that was all," Clare explained. "Cars and horses and women. It wasn't his fault; they never got on, he and his grandmother. She had this crazy idea about those old cavalrymen, and she couldn't understand why Angus didn't see it the way she did. You've seen the hall of their house. How would you like to have been brought up with all those memorials?"

"I wouldn't," Keith answered promptly. "Didn't I hear rumours about her having cut him out of her will?"

"She was always threatening to do it," Anabelle said.

"Could she?" Keith enquired. "That's to say, isn't it in trust?"

"No. Father knows the ins and outs better than I do, but there's some clause about Angus not inheriting until he's thirty."

"Which he will be soon, so she'd better hurry," put in Clare.

"Anyway, he's home," Anabelle said, "and now that the shock of seeing him has died down, I don't care one way or the other—but it's going to be hard on Philip."

"Why so?" Keith asked. "Boyhood enemies or rivals in love?"

"Angus's love affairs were mostly outside the town," Clare said. "To listen to local gossip, you'd have thought he was fathering a child a week, but nobody ever came forward with a complaint—or even with a horsewhip. If you ask me, most of it was old women's tongues wagging."

James stirred, opened his eyes, and seemed about to go to sleep again.

"Don't let him settle down until he's had a drink," advised Anabelle. "Can you find a place to stop?"

Keith chose a quiet side turning; as he stopped the car, John wakened.

"Come on out and have a run," Keith said.

It was almost seven, but there was still warmth in the patches of sunshine that filtered through the trees. They had been traveling without haste; the road between Penafiel and Amarante had not been of sufficient interest or beauty to draw their minds from their own concerns, but when they were once more in the car and on their way, their route lay towards the wild and picturesque Serra do Marão, and they drove in silence, their eyes on the beautiful, swiftly changing scene. They came to the approaches of Vila Real. Keith and Clare had been here only three days earlier, staying in one of the beautiful sixteenth-century palaces; and for some moments he stopped the car on the Terreiro do Calvario and, although they were afraid to get out for fear of disturbing the sleeping boys, they sat gazing in delight at the lovely countryside.

They went past Mateus with its extraordinary palace, its façade familiar to all drinkers of the wine; on to Sabrosa—and now they were nearing Prendergast country. Small, printed route cards were issued in advance to all guests driving to the Quinta for the first time, but Keith was on familiar ground. He had left the main road; the going was rougher and they were climbing steeply—and then came the descent to the

Douro. They passed terraced vineyards and then, in the dusk, a clear view of the Quinta showed above the river. It looked lonely and white and spreading; but as they looked, lights blazed out and gave the house a look of timely welcome.

It was dark when they climbed the winding road and waited for the massive gates to be opened, but the lights of the porch and the noise of the reception by Mr. Prendergast and his brother, Margaret and Dinah, three large dogs, two puppies, a Siamese cat, and several smiling servants brought John and James to wide-awake attention.

Within minutes of their arrival, Keith was seated in a deep chair between the brothers; drinks were beside them. The boys were upstairs and maids were attending to their supper and baths. Clare was unpacking, with Dinah sitting on the bed talking; Margaret was in Anabelle's room, shouting items of news as Anabelle bathed and changed.

Dinner was late and was spread on the marble table on the verandah overlooking the river. When they went into the drawing room after the meal, a fire crackled in the huge chimney. Sitting round it, the guests' programme was outlined for them—dancing, driving, riding and—weather permitting—tennis and swimming.

Clare, in a brief, faded cotton nightdress, strolled into Anabelle's bedroom to say good night.

"Noisy lot," she commented. "I'd forgotten how noisy. But nice." She clambered onto the high, narrow bed Anabelle was to occupy. "Kind of feudal, isn't it? This is the kind of house I'd like."

"This size?"

"No. Much smaller, but homey, like this."

"I'd like to get Mrs. Jansen here and show her people who don't worry about a bit of honest mud on the carpets."

"Did Margaret tell you she was engaged?"

"Yes. And Dinah's on the brink. Why can't she make up her mind?"

"She wants them both. I can see her problem. Speaking of marrying, I've got an idea."

"Well?"

"About Olivia."

Anabelle, putting cream on her face, turned from the glass in surprise.

"Olivia? Show me anybody more capable than Olivia of getting herself married," she challenged. "Who've you got in mind?"

"Angus Pemberton."

For some moments, Anabelle was too surprised to speak. Then:

"You're just fooling," she said. "You can't possibly be serious."

"But I am. He liked playing tricks when we were young, but that was only because he had nothing better to do; he's not the practical-joker type. You said yourself, in the car coming down here, that you don't care one way or the other about his turning up again —which means that you won't carry on any sort of feud. He's a lifelong friend and neighbour and—"

"Friend!"

Clare slipped down from the bed.

"Well, I like him," she said. "If he's free, if he's cooperative, if Olivia likes him—"

"Olivia won't look at him if there's a chance of his going back to Brazil; nobody's going to make her leave London."

"I bet Angus could. I know as well as you do that she's got a string of men to choose from any time she feels like marrying—but I'd like to see her settled."

"So would I—but not with Angus Pemberton."

"Couldn't we at least try to get them together?"

"You try. Leave me out of it."

"Just because he dropped wasps into your tea?"

"Just because. You can put the proposition to Olivia, but you needn't say I agreed to it. I'd as soon . . ."

"As soon what?"

"Since you ask, I'd as soon see her thrown to the wolves."

Chapter Two

Mr. PRENDERGAST and his brother were widowers
—great, shaggy, genial, roaring men who loved to dis-
pense hospitality and who had little or no interest in
events taking place in the world beyond their bounda-
ries. They had not been out of Portugal for forty
years; the *Times* and one or two other English papers
were still delivered regularly and were studied with
interest during the cricket season, but for both Joseph
and George the chief fact of interest regarding their
motherland was that not enough port was being
drunk there. There were intermittent wars in the
world, but the brothers were engaged in one which
was waged ceaselessly—against the producers of
sherry. The old, heavy types of port might be out of
favour, but who, shouted Joseph and George passionately, what fool would drink sherry when he could
get cool, delicate, delicious white port? Try it, my
dear feller; here, have a glass, my dear young lady.

The interests of Dinah and Margaret were also lim-
ited to the Quinta and its neighbourhood. Lazy and
good-natured, they found in their home all the ease
and comfort they wished for, and friends like Anabelle and Clare came out frequently from England to
save them the trouble of going there.

Clare's visit had begun badly, for on the day after
her arrival she was seized by a sharp attack of morn-

ing sickness. The news spread within minutes throughout the household, bringing down a shower of congratulations upon Keith at the breakfast table and causing heated arguments among the maids as to which of them should be the one to attend to the Senhora. John and James were led upstairs by two dusky little girls, all four offering damp handfuls of aromatic herbs. Keith, muttering a confused sentence about women's lot, went out for a walk. Mr. Prendergast, learning of his departure, hurried after him on horseback, leading a horse for his guest. George creaked upstairs, followed by the two largest dogs and the Siamese cat, in his arms a miscellaneous collection of blooms he had himself uprooted from the overgrown, brilliantly coloured wilderness known as the garden. Anabelle moved to the door of Clare's room in time to bar his entrance, and as tactfully as possible indicated that all Clare wanted was to be left alone.

"Quite right; quite right." George lowered his voice to a sympathetic roar. "Bit of quiet, that's all she needs. She ought to sniff those herbs; do her a power of good. My wife went through the same thing more than once; always came to nothing, worse luck. Quiet, that's the thing," he shouted enthusiastically. "And that's one thing we can offer. No traffic, no road drills, no trams or buses and, thank God, no scooters. Tell her to have a good sleep."

He stumbled over a dog, which gave a yelp; recovering, he jostled the Siamese cat, which gave an unearthly scream of protest. The only thing he hadn't done, moaned Clare, was to ring the church bells.

Anabelle, going downstairs to look for John and James, found them at length among the hens and turkeys, accompanied by their guarding shadows and five or six companions of their own age. There was nothing for her to do but choose between accompanying Dinah and Margaret to visit one of their neighbours, or wandering round the grounds by herself.

She chose to stay by herself, and walked slowly past the little white houses of the estate employes, greeting women seated on doorsteps or nursing babies or washing in the communal tank. The sunny peacefulness of the scene soothed her, and she found courage to examine her feelings and to search for the real causes of her quarrel with Philip. It had been the first since their engagement, and it had left her shaken, for she was aware that it had been more than a mere clash of opinions; it had struck an ugly, dissonant note which still echoed in her mind.

It was no use dwelling on it, she decided. Philip would be here in two days. Not having met the Prendergasts before, he would doubtless find them overpowering; but in the general good will and good nature, he might sense something notably missing in the Jansen ménage.

It was the only time she had for reflection until his arrival, for the chief flaw in the Prendergasts' hospitality was their disinclination to leave guests to themselves; if they had wanted to be alone, they argued, why had they come? A visit was a visit, and there was no need to be out all the time; but if not out, then share the family life, give us the pleasure of your society, let's see as much of you as possible before the unwelcome hour comes for your departure. So saying, the brothers tramped in and out with the dogs, leaving trails of dust or mud; friends arrived unexpectedly and were pressed to stay for meals or for weeks; the big dogs curled up on carpets and the smaller ones leapt onto chairs; at all functions, the Siamese cat demanded a large share of attention and yowled dismally if not accorded it. Dinah played jazz records in one room while Margaret thumped a piano in another. The door of the vast room in which the brothers conducted the business of the estate stood open wide, and they themselves were accessible at all times to everybody.

Philip, arriving by car just before a dinner at which more than a dozen guests were present, bore up better than Anabelle had expected. She had almost forgotten the Jansens; their life, stilted and formal, had no relation to this free-and-easy, take-life-as-it-comes atmosphere. She and Keith and the boys were enjoying themselves, and the only check to Clare's pleasure were the uncomfortable morning hours.

The noise after dinner was overpowering, but Mr. Prendergast, seated at ease on a long chair on the verandah between Anabelle and Philip, managed without difficulty to make himself heard.

"Haven't had a chance to congratulate you both," he began, fortissimo. "So many of these young couples about, one gets mixed up—there's Margaret as good as married, and Dinah going off next, and soon there'll be nobody on this place but two lonely old crocks. When're you two going to get married, hey?"

"In July," Anabelle told him.

"Nice month. I was married in July myself. She came out to Oporto and we got married there—nice and quiet, it was; just us and her parents and the consul and a few friends—not more than eighty or ninety, I'd say, because we'd kept it dark. . . . But look here, young feller," he broke off to say indignantly, "don't tell me you're only here for a couple of days. Can't have that. This girl of yours has been mooning for you; you can't run off and desert her."

"I'm afraid I've no choice." Philip's polite, regretful words sounded like the cheeping of birds after a storm. "It's very kind of you."

"Well, if he can't stay, then you've got to," Mr. Prendergast told Anabelle firmly. "Can't have you going when Clare goes. 'Sides, she's going in the other direction—isn't she going to stay in Paris? P'raps you're going too?"

"No. They're going to drive me to Oporto and put me on a train."

"Train? *What?* Stuffy train ride all the way to England? Mustn't dream of it, my dear girl. Out of the question. Tell you what: I'll see if I can fix you up in ten days on the *Yeoman*—she's owned by old Clarkson; you can see him and his wife in there if you look; she's the one holding that squalling cat of ours, and he's the old shock-head beside her. Nice little ship —he's got four of 'em; nothing but barrels of splendid port and nice, comfortable accommodations for twenty or so picked passengers. You've only to say the word. You'd enjoy it, y'know; nobody but old friends on board; good, seaworthy old tubs, fine run of deck space and plenty of bathrooms, and every-body old friends of everybody, as I said. How about it?"

She hesitated. She knew enough to realize that in spite of the casual manner of the invitation, it was a chance that would not come her way again. Neither of the other two alternatives—flying back to Lisbon and thence to England, or going by train—offered anything as interesting.

Her hesitation was enough. Mr. Prendergast bawled to Mr. Clarkson, who came out and listened smilingly to the proposal; he would send to Oporto, he said, for the list, and he would also have a word with the agent, but as far as he knew, the ship wasn't full, and if it wasn't, Miss Baird would certainly be aboard.

"There you are!" said Mr. Prendergast trium-phantly. "You grab your chance and go; they don't run every week by any means, and a lot of people would give their ears and whiskers for a trip on one. . . . Now don't you stay here listening to two old men; go out there into the garden with your young man and get your canoodling done. I can see this young feller's impatient to get you to himself."

They left him and wandered out into the darkness, and for once nobody followed them. The noise grew fainter and at last dropped to a confusion of distant sounds. Philip, halting, drew her into his arms and kissed her. She had never thought him passionate, but with the new, disturbing clear-sightedness that seemed to have grown out of their quarrel, his em-brace seemed like that of a nervous youth in a ball-room.

"I'm sorry about those ghastly two weeks," she said impulsively. "I—"

"Well, they're over," he said. "I don't think the Jansens will hold it against us."

Panic seized her. The words were bad enough; the smug tone in which they were uttered drove straight through to her nerves and set them quivering. She drew herself slowly out of his arms.

"Could you stop thinking about the Jansens and start thinking about me?" she asked quietly.

He laughed.

"Think about you? I've done nothing else since you left Lisbon. Did you think I didn't miss you?"

"I missed you too. But perhaps," she suggested, "this is as good a time as any to decide just how much the Jansens are going to matter in our lives."

"But good heavens, Anabelle, they're my—"

"—Chief and his wife. I know. As such, I'm prepared to be polite and refrain from doing anything to antagonize them. I'll admire their furniture and their china; I'll gasp in wonder when Mrs. Jansen tells me what it all cost. I'll thank her profusely for all her patronage . . . but I won't do more than that. We'll be married in two months, and I want to help you in every way I can—but there's a difference between respect for one's employers and this servile attitude you've fallen into. Let's agree, here and now, that the Jansens, he and she both, are cheap, vulgar, get-rich-quick nobodys. Let's admit that working for them offers great opportunities, for which we're prepared to overlook their deficiencies—but don't, don't, don't let's keep up this farce about what sort of people they really are. You can't *like* them, can you? You can't point out one single instance of good sense—and I don't mean money sense—in either of them, can you? Can you?"

There was a pause. She hoped that he was thinking over what she had said—but when he spoke, it was only to prove that he had scarcely listened.

"When you left," he said, "I had a long talk with both of them. They liked you, Anabelle; they really liked you. I won't say they didn't have reservations, but considering what they'd just been through, wondering for two whole weeks how much damage those boys might have done, I don't blame them. They said some very nice things about you. They . . ."

Inexplicably he paused. She waited, staring past his shoulder at the brilliant lights of the house and struggling to subdue her sense of foreboding. He had not, she realized suddenly, been completely at ease when he arrived. His greeting to her had been affectionate but guarded; she had put it down to the overpowering presence of the Prendergast family and their friends, but now she was certain that he had arrived with something on his mind—something that affected their future. In spite of this conviction, she found it impossible to believe that a couple like the Jansens could say or do anything that could seriously affect her future with Philip.

"There was something I wanted to say," he began.

"Well then, say it."

She did her best to keep the words free from any suggestion of sharpness; she wanted to heal and not to widen the breach between them.

"You may not like this," he said. "That is, you may feel that I should have looked at it solely from your point of view—but what I've got to keep in mind, always, is the fact that my job's all-important. My mother, as you know, lives on alimony. When she dies, there'll be nothing but my job, and perhaps the house, if it isn't mortgaged, which I rather suspect it is. I know there are things about the Jansens that annoy you, but going along with them means a lot to me. I'm the only man on this job. If I can keep in with them, I'll be in charge of a chain of offices from Lisbon to Milan. They've offered to let me come in on a partnership basis, which means that in a couple of years' time I'll be earning a good deal more than most men of my age. Once I've opened up the branch in Rome next month, and—"

"Next month?"

"Yes. That's what I was coming to. I told the Jansens I'd put it to you—and of course, what you say, I shall abide by. But I don't need to tell you that—"

"They want you to go to Rome next month?"

"That was the idea."

"For how long?"

"Well, they quite saw that if I went, it would take me three or four months to get the thing on its feet. They—"

"They asked you to put off your . . . our . . . wedding?"

"They didn't put it quite like that, Anabelle; don't make them out worse than they are. They quite saw my difficulty. They said that they left it entirely up to you."

"That's to say, you told them you would agree, if I would agree, to put off the date of our wedding?"

"That's exactly it. I wouldn't have taken a step like that without consulting you. Whatever you decided, I told them quite frankly and firmly, I would abide by."

Silence fell. He was content to wait; the proposal had not been easy to make, but he had made it. The bridge was crossed.

For Anabelle, the moment was one of more than humiliation. They had been engaged for a year, out of which he had been away more than eight months. She had, in agreeing to marry him, brushed aside or ignored the wishes and opinions of all those nearest to her. He had, she was well aware, never been liked in Steyne—but she had always been convinced that, to her, he showed a side that others never saw. He had been handicapped all his life by a mother who was never without a train of husbands, past and present; laying the blame for all Philip's shortcomings at her door, Anabelle had ranged herself on his side in many battles throughout their childhood; her engagement, she was beginning to understand, had been a practical extension of this partisanship. And she was even more clearly aware that she had been content with his long-drawn-out, passionless courtship only because she had had no strong desire to change her life. She had been satisfied with things as they were, with him as he was: tall, good-looking, gentle . . . and undemanding.

Standing in the darkness, she thought suddenly of her father. She had never believed him to be a force in the lives of his children, but she would have given much at this moment to hear his quiet, flat, level voice and listen to his reluctantly given opinions. But her father was at Steyne—and Philip was here, and he had asked her to postpone their wedding because Mr. and Mrs. Jansen . . .

She heard herself speaking in a tone which, to her relief, sounded calm and reasonable.

"It isn't my decision, Philip; it's your own. The Jansens have known for over a year that we'd fixed July for our wedding. They said nothing to you about opening new branches before I went to stay with them—did they?"

"As a matter of fact, no; they—"

"They didn't like me, and this is their way of saying so."

"That's nonsense, Anabelle. There's nothing personal about this; it's simply a business proposal. I'd have to be at home for at least a week before the wedding, and I couldn't ask for less than two weeks for our honeymoon. That makes three weeks' delay, as Mr. Jansen pointed out—three weeks at the most crucial time. If we put it off until the end of the year—"

"Do you want to?"

"Haven't I just said that it's up to you?"

"If I said that it was now—July—or never, what would you say?"

"Well, frankly, I'd be disappointed. Disappointed in you, I mean. I'd be quite prepared for my mother to react like that—what's one scene more or less to my mother? But you . . . I would have said you had a more sane outlook."

"What's saner than a desire to get married at the time that was fixed?"

"Nothing. Nothing whatsoever. But you're not dealing with a man who could have any ulterior motive. I—"

"Ulterior motive?"

"Don't pretend you don't understand." The peevish note was back. "What I mean is that putting off a wedding might sound suspicious in some cases, but you know very well that I've never looked at any other woman but you. Not seriously, that is. All I want you to do is think over Mr. Jansen's proposal and give me your decision before I leave."

She could, she knew, give him her decision now. She would have put off her wedding for any reasonable reasons, but she could not accept the intrusion of the Jansens into a matter which so intimately concerned Philip and herself. She tried to banish all petty considerations from her mind, but all she could see was the picture of Philip listening with courteous attention to a proposal which sounded to her nothing short of insolent.

The lights of a car flashed across the pool of darkness in which they were standing. Another visitor. Somebody else to enjoy the Prendergasts' uncomplicated hospitality; somebody else to be absorbed into the good-hearted household.

She spoke calmly.

"I'll think it over," she said.

"Good girl."

She had nothing to add, and he seemed to sense that she was not in a mood for demonstrations of affection. They walked in silence towards the house, and the noise grew in volume and drew from Philip a petulant protest.

"I don't think I could stand this clatter for long."

"You won't have to."

"Are you going to take up that offer of going home by sea?"

"I don't know. I'll think that over too."

He turned to study her expression by the light streaming from the house, but there was no time for him to speak. From the verandah came Mr. Prendergast's now familiar roar.

"Well, there you are, you two. Come along, come along and see who we've got here for you. An old friend. Somebody who's anxious to say hello and have a chat about old times. Come along, come up here and meet somebody you used to play with not so long ago."

Perhaps she and Philip were both too much absorbed in their present problem to have any premonition. They stepped onto the verandah to confront a familiar figure that emerged from the shadow cast by their host's huge frame.

"Here he is," shouted Mr. Prendergast. "Just turned up, and going to stay as long as we can keep him from running away. Your old friend Angus Pemberton."

Angus, smiling, friendly, and at ease, said casually

that it was nice to see them again—and Anabelle was surprised to find herself in cordial agreement with the sentiment. He could not, she thought gratefully, have appeared at a more opportune moment; his presence afforded the most appropriate form of retribution for Philip, whose chagrin was only too evident. It was balm to her smarting feelings to see him reduced by Angus, in three easy sentences, to impotent rage.

"I didn't know you knew Angus," she said to Mr. Prendergast.

"Matter of fact, first time we've met," Mr. Prendergast explained. "He's been staying with some old friends of mine, and when he rang up to say he knew old Kemp over in Rio, why, come along at once, my dear chap, I said; come along and stay and have a chat and tell us how the old feller's faring out there; bring your bags and settle down for a visit—and so here he is, and now he tells me you were born next door to one another and were childhood sweethearts—isn't that extraordinary?"

"Yes," Anabelle said. "It is."

"Now take him along and find the girls and see that they make him comfortable—his room's ready. I'll take care of this fiancé of yours till you get back."

She led Angus round the edge of the drawing room which, with its two great carpets rolled aside, had been turned into a ballroom. Young couples were facing one another in the centre, their bodies jerking to the music; round them revolved the elderly and the sedate in the style of an earlier day.

In the hall, Angus glanced at his clothes.

"Quick bath, quick change," he said. "Can I have the third from this one?"

"I'll find Dinah and Margaret," she said.

As she turned to go in search of them, Clare came into the hall and stopped, astounded.

"Angus? No! Optical illusion," she decided.

Angus kissed her warmly.

"Lovelier than ever," he declared with obvious sincerity. "Why didn't you wait for me?"

"Angus darling, I thought you were dead, and so I

got married." She disengaged herself and looked round for Keith. "Hey, Keith!"

The two men shook hands, clearly pleased with one another.

"Is this a sort of prodigal-grandson act you're staging?" Keith asked.

"I'm going home to knock some sense into my grandmother—she's talking of disinheriting me," Angus said frankly.

"I gather it's not a new threat."

"This time it sounded more serious."

Keith smiled.

"If I know her, she'll do what she wants to do."

"She has done so far," Angus admitted, "but we mustn't let it grow into a habit."

He turned to greet Dinah and Margaret, and they led him up to his room.

"Who invited him?" Clare asked when they had gone.

"He invited himself; more accurately, he got himself invited," Anabelle said.

"Wonder why?" Keith mused.

Angus, when asked later, supplied a convincing series of answers. He had wanted, before leaving Portugal, to see Mr. Prendergast and his brother, of whom, in Brazil, he had heard so much. He wanted to meet Keith, whom he had never seen; here, moreover, so conveniently assembled under one roof, were Anabelle and Clare and Philip, to say nothing of Clare's little boys, of whose arrival in the world nobody had troubled to inform him. He had been longing to meet Dinah and Margaret again. And he had—he had almost forgotten—several friendly messages to deliver from Mr. Kemp in Brazil. He had also wanted, of course, to fill in gaps in the news of Steyne in general and his grandmother in particular.

But he had no need to advance reasons for coming; it was clear that the Prendergasts were delighted to have him; they were unanimous in voting him the ideal guest: handsome, pleasant, fond of children and dogs, able to explain his needs to the servants without an interpreter, good on a horse, splendid on a dance floor . . . and a good judge of port.

Nobody considered Philip's feelings. He would have liked to find someone, anyone, to whom he could have hinted his disability to share in the general approbation; someone who could perhaps have shared, discreetly, his own unfavourable opinion—but nobody asked his opinion. His disparaging remarks drew no response whatsoever from Anabelle; Clare, as usual, snubbed him.

Left to himself—for there were few opportunities for being alone with Anabelle, none of which she availed herself—he had time to realize that the proposition of postponing the wedding, which had seemed so reasonable when broached by Mr. and Mrs. Jansen, had somehow misfired. Anabelle refused further discussion; he must go back and discuss the matter once more with the Jansens, she said, and if they decided on postponement, to postponement she would agree —but there was something in the tone in which she had said it that left him far from reassured.

He left early on Monday morning, but even then there was no chance of being alone with Anabelle; the Prendergasts were early risers and were not only present at the earlier than usual breakfast but also assembled in strength in the hall, with dogs, cats, and servants, to give him a send-off.

When he had gone, Anabelle went up to Clare's room, to find her sitting up in bed with a tray on her knees, finishing breakfast.

"Keith tells me you're all right this morning," she said.

"So far," Clare said. "Philip gone?"

"Yes. The entire family had breakfast with us."

"Serves him right. You ought to tell him, next time you get him alone, that a guest's first duty is to look as though he's enjoying himself. Why does he moon about the way he does? Why doesn't he mix?"

"He wasn't feeling social. We started off by having a row."

"What about?"

Anabelle told her, and Clare listened without comment.

"So that's why he looked so fiddle-faced," she said at the end.

"That, and Angus Pemberton."

"Keith likes Angus; he says he's all right—and Keith's a good judge. He thinks he'll do well for Olivia."

"That makes it practically a certainty; all you have to do now is tell Angus and Olivia that it's been arranged."

"Time enough; Angus keeps saying he's home for good. If Philip tells you that these Jansens still want him to put off the wedding, what'll you do?"

"At this moment I feel I'd gladly put it off. For ever. But I'm trying to be fair; if I'd stayed at home, if I hadn't come out to Lisbon and met the Jansens, if Philip had written a letter to say that Mr. Jansen wanted him to open the Rome office straightaway, everything would have been different. I would have believed it all. But now I don't. I've met them, and I'm quite certain this idea was born in Mrs. Jansen's brain and then put to her husband. They're both pretty awful, but she's awfuller than he is. She didn't like me to begin with; when she found that I had ideas of my own, she liked me even less. They've got Philip just where it suits them. For all I know, they may be genuinely fond of him; they've no family, and there might be a touch of this son-we-might-have-had attitude. But about their feelings towards me, I'm in no doubt whatsoever: they're both as sick as anything because Philip's going to marry a woman they won't be able to boss."

"Has he gone back to say you won't?"

"No. He's merely going to say I don't want to."

"Well, if I were you, I'd make hay. I'd agree to put off the wedding—for ever, as you said. I don't like him. Look: first his mother, then Mrs. Jansen, then you—all trying to make him make up his own mind. He never will, Anabelle. All his life he'll be shouting for help because he has to have someone to decide for

him. It's funny that men like that always fall in love
with women like you."

"What's the matter with women like me?"

"I didn't say there was anything the matter with
them. Don't get mad. I only meant that you've got
this soft streak, and it worries me because I think that
—deep down—you've got exactly the same opinion of
Philip as most of the rest of us; but because you're
sorry for him, you've added up his good qualities, if
any, and thrown in an extra percentage to screw
yourself up into marrying him."

"Isn't that more or less what everybody has to do
before deciding to marry somebody?"

"No. At least not to the extent that you've done it.
The very fact that you can think clearly enough to do
all this weighing and measuring shows that there's
something wrong. Take me: now that I've come to, I
look at Keith and wonder how I ever had the sense to
see beyond his comic-strip countenance—but at the
time, I didn't even know he had a countenance. I
didn't marry him out of kindness. Something hit me,
and I woke up in hospital and heard the nurse saying
it was a fine little boy. See what I mean?"

"Yes, I see. Seeing doesn't help much."

"With a disposition like yours, you're bound to
keep hitting trouble. Me, I always believed that being
frank at the start—all right, being ruddy rude if you
like—saved a whole lot of bother later. Olivia's different again—she doesn't say anything out loud, but
all the same she knows what she wants, and she gets it
simply by helping herself if it's available. You, having
this nice nature, get stuck with Philip. Keith says
you've got a good brain and sound judgment and you
work things out to a reasonable conclusion—and then
you wash it all down the drain because you don't
want to hurt anybody. Well, coming back to the
matter in hand, if you don't hurt Philip now, this
Mrs. Jansen will. One more small point: they may be
awful, but they're Philip's bread and butter; if you're
going to marry him, you'll have to keep that in mind."

"He *crawls*."

"Didn't he always? Did he ever once, in all his life,

hit back? Not he. He always had ten good reasons for
not punching another boy on the nose when another
boy had punched him on the nose. You can't change
people; people are what they are. These Jansens are
what they are, and you'll have to learn to live with
them. They've got their own case: they invite you out
to Lisbon because they want to take a look at you;
you, far from arriving wearing your best dress and a
meek expression, show up with two small boys—for
which I'm grateful; don't think I'm not. You arrive
with John and James, the Jansens show they don't
like it, so you show you don't like them, so they
show they don't like you. So they try to get their
own back."

"So Philip has to go on crawling?"

"No. Wait and see what happens when he gets
back to Lisbon. In the meantime—"

In the meantime, there was a thundering on the
door, followed by the entrance of Dinah with two
dogs.

"Clare, Keith said you were feeling all right—are
you coming to the fair?"

"What fair?" Clare enquired.

"It's about eight miles away, at a little village called
Virgilio; we're going to take a picnic and . . . Get *off*
that bed, you big brute. Push him off, Clare. *Bother!*
Now he's put his great foot on your tray. Never
mind; here, let me take it. Would you both like to
come?"

Clare, mopping coffee stains from the sheets and
from her nightdress, said that she could be ready in
twenty minutes. Anabelle, picking pieces of toast off
the rug, said that she liked nothing better than a fair,
and helped to get the dogs out into the corridor.

Virgilio proved to be a cluster of little red-roofed
houses ringed by pine woods. There had been a threat
of rain, but when the three Prendergast cars, loaded
with guests, servants, and children, arrived shortly
after eleven o'clock, the sun was shining warmly.
Anabelle, walking between Dinah and Mr. Prendergast towards the fairground, found the colours almost
blinding. There were stalls so numerous that it was

difficult to pick a way through them; vendors sat on the ground beside baskets piled with picturesque vegetables; embroidered cloths were spread out for inspection, food simmered in pots on fires, hens clacked, donkeys brayed, old women swathed in black sat watchfully eyeing babies in improvised cradles.

The Prendergasts were already buying. Clare and Keith had wandered away, taking Angus as interpreter; Dinah and Margaret were claimed by a party of friends. Anabelle freed the maid who was in charge of John and James, and the girl, with a grateful, flashing smile, darted away. Looking after the boys, never a problem, was here only too easy, for on the fringe of the fairground were pigs and poultry and goats to be inspected.

Happy but hot, the three withdrew after a time to the shelter of the pines. Here were more animals; here also were the exhausted and the elderly—among the latter a group that drew Anabelle's attention as she passed them: an old man seated in a wheel chair, a male attendant, and a small thin old priest. With them was a boy of about James's age; as they passed, he turned to stare, and began to walk slowly beside them, heedless of the murmured admonition of the attendant.

"Hello," offered James. "What's your name?"

They had all halted. The attendant had moved forward and was hesitating, uncertain of the newcomer's welcome. But the boy, confident and suddenly smiling, had joined Anabelle and the boys.

"I speak English," he announced. "I can know what you are saying. My name is Luis Antonio Jose Ribeiro. I have five years. How are you called?"

The question, surprisingly, was addressed to Anabelle. She withdrew her attention from his beautiful natural silk suit and fixed it on his face. It was oval, with a glowing, dark peach skin, a small nose, curving mouth, and—she studied them in delight—large, beautiful, thick-lashed, intelligent brown eyes.

"My name is Anabelle Evelyn Baird," she told him. "This is James Keith Antrobus Trevor. This is his brother John Evelyn Trevor."

The boy frowned.

"Both . . . Eve-lyn? Lady and little boy too?"

"Yes, I'm afraid so, Luis. It's very confusing, but that's the way it is," Anabelle explained. She glanced at the group the boy had left. "We're on our way to see some of those donkeys over there. Would you like to come too?"

"Yes." Without the slightest hesitation, he stepped up and took her hand. "Let us go."

"But you must ask if you may come."

"He"—a small brown hand gestured toward the attendant—"he will come too."

"I don't think there's any need for that," Anabelle said firmly. "Tell him I'll bring you back soon. In fact, you'd better tell your . . . your grandfather?"

"Yes. My grandfather." A rapid order in Portuguese ensured that Grandfather would get the message. "Come." He held out his free hand to James. "We shall go."

They walked up the slope; glancing back, Anabelle saw the eyes of the old man and the priest fixed on herself; if she had had any Portuguese, she reflected, she would have warned them about letting a little boy who looked as valuable as this little boy go off with total strangers. Put a little cocked hat on that arrogant head, put him in long boots, and hand him a dagger, and there was one of your old-time fairy-story illustrations.

He didn't, it appeared, want to play—not with the animals, not with James or John. He settled on a fallen pine beside Anabelle and said that he wished to talk.

"About England. I have never been, but I am going soon," he said. "My grandfather is sending me soon."

"Really? Where are you going to stay?" Anabelle enquired.

He shrugged. John and James, staring, lost in admiration, tried to lift their shoulders in the same brief, casual, graceful gesture, and failed altogether; going on trying kept them absorbed for some time.

"I do not know where; but England is small, like Portugal—not?"

"Is," agreed Anabelle. "Are you going to stay with relations?"

"With a friend, my grandfather said. Perhaps I will see you?"

She tried to imagine him in England but without much success; seated beside her, ignoring John and James, his air calm and entirely poised, he did not fit into any small-boy category she knew. Her attempts to interest him in any of the things that experience had shown her to be popular with John and James met with as little success as their attempts at shrugging; he did not, he said politely, want to play; he wished only to hear about England.

"You have a big house?" he enquired.

"No; a small one."

"How many divisions?"

"Rooms? Drawing room, dining room, five bedrooms, one and a half bathrooms—that is, one bath and one shower—and the usual hall and cloakroom. A small garden, mostly vegetables because my father likes growing vegetables. And a nice view of the sea."

He did not seem impressed.

"You have other little boys?"

"I haven't any little boys. In fact, I'm not married. John and James are my nephews."

"Your—?"

"My sister's children."

"Please say that word again."

"Nephews?"

"Thank you."

They were interrupted, to her disappointment, by a hail from Clare. They all went to meet her, and she studied Luis admiringly.

"He speaks English," Anabelle put in before there was time to comment.

"My grandfather taught me. You are the sister that has these boys?" Luis asked.

"I am. Who do you belong to?" asked Clare.

"I'm just taking him back to his grandfather," Anabelle explained.

"Pity. Well, I'll take John and James; Keith's discovered an old lady who knew him when he was *so* high, and she wants to inspect his family. I'll meet you somewhere near the cars."

Anabelle, walking on with Luis, saw the priest coming towards her. Luis did not release her hand.

"His name is Father Vicento," he said. "He is our priest."

Father Vicento joined them and gave a stiff little bow. Then he addressed Luis in Portuguese.

"He says," translated Luis, "that my grandfather asks that you speak with him. He is old and his legs are weak and he cannot walk, so he cannot come to you."

As Anabelle walked between Father Vicento and Luis towards the wheel chair, the old man's eyes, keen and unblinking, did not leave her. As she stopped before him, he bent his frail old body in a bow and then looked up at her with a faint smile.

"You are very kind," he said gently, in halting but correct English. "I wished to thank you."

She smiled.

"Thank me? I enjoyed meeting Luis. He tells me he's going to England."

The faded old eyes rested on Luis, who was talking to the priest.

"I hope that he will go soon. But there is—there is serious opposition to his going. If I can, I will send him." His eyes rested on hers. "The little boys with you, they are—?"

"My nephews," she supplied.

"They look very well and very happy. And you yourself—you seem to like children. Perhaps you do not like all children?"

"Who does? I daresay there are little devils in Portugal as well as in England," Anabelle said with a smile. "My trouble is that I usually like the little devils better than the little angels."

She saw a responsive smile on Father Vicento's face; if he did not speak English, he could at least follow the trend of her remarks.

"Your nephews are splendid little boys. They live with you?" asked the old man.

His questions were put with gentle hesitation;

sometimes he paused—whether for breath or for the right word in English, she could not judge.

"They live with me when their mother goes away. When she has to go away with her husband, the boys come to me."

His eyes were on her engagement ring.

"But when you marry . . . When will you marry?"

"Perhaps in July. Perhaps"—to her amazement, the words were out before she could check them—"perhaps not at all."

"That . . ."

He paused, and this time she knew why. His hand, gripping the side of the chair, gave the only other indication—but she knew that he was fighting for breath.

"Look," she broke in impulsively, "you shouldn't be talking."

There was no mistaking the meaning of the words he spoke in reply; they were uttered quietly, but his eyes conveyed their meaning.

"There is not much time to talk, Miss Baird."

For a few moments, she could not speak; she was struggling against a feeling of unreality. The encounter with Luis, the grave attendant, the sober priest, the old man—if he had said so aloud, she could not have understood more clearly that he was dying—seemed to close in and isolate her from the sights and the sounds of the fair. His quiet voice seemed to come from a distance. His eyes held hers for a long moment.

"I wished to see you. I wished to speak with you. Now I am satisfied."

She saw, with the same sense of timelessness, that Luis had put out his hand and given her a stiff, meant-to-be-English handshake. The priest bowed. The old man took her hand, pressed it gently, and released it; as she turned away, the attendant had taken hold of the chair back and was wheeling the old man away.

The drive home with Mr. Prendergast, Clare, and Angus Pemberton did nothing to rid her of her sense of unreality. Her efforts to discover whether Mr.

Prendergast had noticed the group met with a total lack of response.

"Old feller in a wheel chair? Priest? Small boy and servant? Well, now. Priest, yes; see them every day and everywhere. Little boy—six or so in every family. But a wheel chair . . . now that's different. Can't say I've ever seen a wheel chair in all my years in Portugal. Daresay you'd see them around Lisbon or Oporto, of course, but up and down these slopes wouldn't encourage anybody to trust themselves in one. Sure you mean a wheel chair?"

"Not an invalid chair—just a chair on wheels. He looked very ill."

"And spoke English, you said?"

"Very good English. The little boy's was shaky, but the old man spoke very well."

"What was the name again?"

"Luis Antonio Jose . . . and then something that sounded like bearer."

"Ribeiro probably. I know dozens of Ribeiros, but there isn't an English-speaking old man—not a well-bred sort of chap, as this one of yours sounds—among 'em. And most certainly not a wheel chair. What was the priest's name?"

"Father Vicento."

"Ah. Dozens of those too. Tell you what: I'll ask old George if he can place them."

"It's not important," Anabelle said.

Even as she spoke, she had a feeling—undefined but strong—that it was very important indeed. Her mind was still full of the strange encounter with the dying old man—for dying she was certain he was. She could dismiss everything but the fact that he had known her name—that, and the expression in his eyes as he had been speaking to her. She could still see the look clearly. It had been an appeal—unvoiced but urgent.

An appeal—for what? What had he said? Very little. He had wished to see her—why? Having seen her, he had expressed himself satisfied—equally, why?

There was less and less hope of finding an answer. George knew nothing of the group, and even after the two brothers had painstakingly run a mental finger down the long list of their Ribeiro acquaintances, they found no boy who answered Luis's description, no man who could have been the boy's grandfather. There emerged a Father Vicento, but he was old and fat and had a parish some miles distant on the other side of the river.

"Why did it stick in your mind?" Keith asked her when they found themselves alone in the drawing room before dinner. "Was it anything special?"

Much as she liked him, she could not bring herself to tell him the childish-sounding truth.

"I liked the little boy," she said. "And the old man was . . . unusual."

"The fact that Mr. Prendergast and his brother couldn't call them to mind means that they must have come in from some way away. The wheel chair was obviously for getting round the fairground. If you were so deeply interested, couldn't you have done some of the questioning, instead of leaving it all to the old man?"

"I suppose you'll laugh, but while it was actually going on, I . . ."

"Go on," he encouraged. "If you put it into words, it might clarify itself."

"The only words I can put it into sound pretty silly. I can only tell you that I had a peculiar feeling —as though I'd floated away from the fair and come down again in a quite different place."

He studied her.

"You ought to have been a journalist too," he commented.

"Why?"

"Because you've sensed a story. I wish I'd been with you."

"So do I. You could have asked him how it was he knew my name."

"That's easy; there weren't many foreigners at the fair, and certainly no others that looked like you. He had only to ask."

"I suppose you'd think I was crazy if I said that I got the idea that he tried to get some sort of message across to me?"

"Political?"

"No."

"You sound sure, but what else could it have been?"

"I don't know—but there was nothing frightened or furtive about any of them. Except for the odd feeling I was left with, they were just a rather interesting old man and a beautiful—because he *was* beautiful— little boy."

"A number of them are. Ten or fifteen years later, in the majority of cases, it's gone. But you've got my nose twitching; would you like to take a run with me tomorrow and see if we can pick up the trail?"

"No, thank you." She spoke decisively. "It's all over —over, anyway, from my end. If he wants anything, he knows my name and he probably knows where to find me. As far as I'm concerned, there's no trail."

"Just as you say." He let it go. "Clare tells me you had a row with Philip."

She frowned.

"Row? It was worse than a row. It was a complete—"

"—cleavage of opinion? You'll come across a lot of those in married life. Won't she?" he asked Angus, who had just strolled into the room.

"Won't she what?"

"Well, you're not in a position to comment," Keith remembered. "I was talking about the occasional sweet disagreements of marriage. Anabelle had a row with Philip."

"*Another* row?" Angus asked with raised eyebrows. "Tck, tck, tck. Do we," he went on, looking speculatively down at a loaded tray, "help ourselves to drinks, or are we to await our hosts?"

"We help ourselves," said Keith, getting up and doing so. "What'll you have, Anabelle?"

"Sherry, please."

"Kindly remember where you are," Angus admonished her in a grave voice.

"Oh, sorry. White port."

"How," Keith asked, handing it to her, "does Angus happen to know so much about your private life?"

"He creeps up and listens to my private conversations, that's how. Just as he used to creep up on the other side of the wall and listen to—"

"Oh, wait now!" Angus broke in protestingly. "Keith, she's misleading you. I had, in those days, a retreat in my own, that's to say my own grandmother's, garden. I'd go there—retreat there—and lie looking up at the treetops meditating, doing nobody any harm—and then? From the other side of the wall, girlish giggles, empty declarations from enamoured young men, and other disclosures which I found extremely embarrassing. Sometimes I bore with it all; at other times I was forced to get up and look over the wall and remonstrate."

"But never, you note, never forced to get up and go away and mind his own business," Anabelle pointed out.

"*She* resented my appearances." Angus waved his glass towards her. "Clare, on the other hand, used to value my advice."

"So she told me." Keith laughed. "It wasn't easy to get a clear picture of you. Clare had one view and Anabelle another. I tried to arrive at a mean."

"Mean is the word," Anabelle said. "Why are people expected to wash out every blot on the back pages just because someone announces they've turned over a new leaf?"

"My, such imagery!" Keith said admiringly. "But does a fellow have to carry around his blots for ever?"

"She's thinking of Milton," Angus said. " 'The childhood shows the man, As morning shows the day'—or words to that effect. If I agreed with that, would I be going to see my grandmother again? No, I wouldn't. But I remind myself that she's nearly seventy-three and may have learned sense—and so I'm going home to find out. I shan't, like Anabelle, dig up old corpses; I shall look forward and not backward. Also, I shall be available if Anabelle should need any advice on how to deal with these constant quarrels with her fiancé."

"Thank you," said Anabelle.

He turned to her.

"I understand Philip better than you do," he pointed out. "Weren't we both, he and I, brought up by difficult, not to say peculiar, women? Where *is* his mother now, incidentally?"

"In Greece. She'll be home for the wedding."

"She ought to know about weddings," Keith commented. "I rather like her, in spite of the husbands. I like your grandmother too."

"I like her myself—at times," Angus said. "It's only on one matter that she's unfortunately unbalanced; apart from that, she's impressive to look at and she's a genuine museum piece; she talks, thinks, and behaves as people would have done if there had been no large-scale wars and no social revolutions. What she was born, she is and ever shall be. When you're with her, you don't have to put the clock back; hers stopped fifty years ago."

"I'd like to have seen her when she was young," Keith said. "She—"

A call from Clare, coming from the garden, stopped him.

"Keith! Come and look. Two lovely green lizards."

He rose and put down his glass.

"I'd better look at green lizards before I drink that," he said.

Left with Angus, Anabelle studied him. He looked tanned and fit.

"When you left Steyne," she asked him, "why did you choose Brazil?"

"I always liked the sound of it. It seemed an exciting sort of country—and so it is. It's got its problems, but what nation hasn't? I like the life—sophisticated or simple, just as you prefer. I like the people. I like the women. I like the scenery and the climate and the music. Particularly the music. In fact, I like Brazil."

"You said you might stay at home for good. What about your job out there?"

"It's there if I want to go back—but I felt that the most important job, just at present, was to go home and see that my grandmother wasn't contemplating any financial foolishness. As you know already, this threat of cutting me out of her will has hung over me most of my life; what's new is my feeling that it's worth doing something to stop her before she goes too far. . . . What made you stay in Steyne? My grandmother, or falling in love with Ancell?"

"I thought of going to London, but I didn't particularly want to. Then your grandmother said she'd like me to go and help her with her accounts, and with her housekeeping, and so I went. Then Clare got engaged, and then she began leaving the children with me, and so . . ."

It didn't, she thought, sound exciting. It sounded singularly dull—but dull or not, she had found it a pleasant life.

"Pleasant—and secure," Angus said with uncanny insight into her thoughts. "Does your father still write textbooks?"

"Not new ones; he revises the old ones."

They were silent; it was, Anabelle thought, the first-ever companionable silence between them. Looking across at him as he sat relaxed, drink in hand, she found that most of her old antagonism had abated—but she was still on her guard; he looked handsome and harmless, but there was still much that she could not fathom behind his dark eyes. The short time he had been a guest of the Prendergasts had shown her that he had no need to run after women; almost without exception, they ran after him. Steyne had judged him harshly; it was too soon to decide whether or not the wagging tongues had lied. At this moment, she was inclined to think they had—but she was still not ready to accept him at Clare or Keith's valuation.

Mr. Prendergast came into the room in the snow-white shirt, black drooping tie, black trousers, and black cummerbund that constituted his evening attire. He beamed at Anabelle.

"All fixed," he said. "You're on the *Yeoman*. I've just had a phone call from Clarkson; you're in a two-berth, but he'll see to it that you get somebody as charming as yourself in with you. I'm going to drive you as far as the Clarksons' and they'll take you on to Oporto. You sail from there—from Leixoes, rather—on Tuesday week." He peered at her glass, took it, and refilled it. "And something else," he added. "I asked about the old man—Ribeiro; I told Clarkson you'd taken a fancy to him. He said he was minister of something or other about thirty years ago; fine chap, good background. His wife died recently, and Clarkson says the old man won't last long. He said they lived in an old place I forget where; no lack of money, he thought."

His loud, practical, factual tone had the effect of robbing the incident of most of the interest it had roused in Anabelle. With the matter thus reduced to the level of a rich old man accompanying his grandson to a fair and making an effort to exchange courtesies with an English girl who had exchanged courtesies with his grandson, she felt she had given it an importance it had never possessed.

But at night in her room, when the door closed on the household, when she lay in the darkness recalling the details of the meeting, it was not so easy to dismiss it so lightly, not so easy to persuade herself that her encounter with Luis's grandfather had been a casual one.

But casual or not, the whole thing, she decided, was over.

Chapter Three

ANGUS WAS THE FIRST to leave the Quinta—to pay, he said, one more visit before going home. He parted lightly from Clare and Keith and Anabelle. Were they not, he pointed out, to meet at Steyne in a very short time?

His going left a bigger gap than Anabelle had anticipated. A man who seldom raised his voice, whose manner was leisurely and relaxed, he had not troubled to compete with the Prendergast gusto—but he had managed, in the course of his casual contacts with his hosts, to establish a firm base for friendship, and his departure left both brothers with a sense of loss. Dinah and Margaret mourned him openly; their men friends, on the other hand, bore up remarkably well.

For Anabelle, the loss was chiefly a visual one: the pace, the noise, the variety of life with the Prendergasts had made her long frequently for the peace of her own home; and at these moments, the sight of Angus Pemberton at ease in a deep chair, drink or book in hand, ready to listen, ready to join in conversation or games or outings, but always with a slight air of detachment, had brought her a measure of relief. He was a spectator; his glance, even when serious, seemed to hold a hint of quiet amusement—sardonic amusement, she thought. She had had few personal encounters with him, but he had been a pleasant and reassuring reminder that beyond the Quinta was a

world in which people could make themselves heard
without using megaphones.

Clare and Keith were the next to go—and with
their departure, most of Anabelle's pleasure in the visit
came to an end and she looked forward to her journey home on the *Yeoman*. There had been no word
from Philip, no telephone call, no letter. She could
have got in touch with him without difficulty, but she
felt that in the circumstances the first move should
come from him. Uneasiness at the lack of news became anger at the thought that he could delay over a
matter which she felt to be of such vital importance
to them both.

Not until the day she left the Quinta did she receive
the letter she was expecting. The car had already set
off, Mr. Prendergast at the wheel, herself seated beside
him, her luggage at the back. On the steps of the house
they had left Dinah and Margaret, George, and the
now familiar assembly of servants. The animals had
run behind the car for some distance; the last view of
the cat had been that of a cream and sable figure claw-
ing its way up a tree. At the fork of the road, they
passed another car going in the opposite direction; it
stopped, and out of one of the windows an arm waved
peremptorily.

"That's old Masters; expect he's picked up some
mail for us," said Mr. Prendergast, putting on the
brakes.

He walked back and met an elderly man holding a
sheaf of letters; taking them, he waved off the other
car and returned to his own.

"Just as I said; letters," he told Anabelle, sorting
them. "Three for you; lucky we didn't start earlier,
or we'd have missed them."

Her father, Philip's mother—the postmark was
London—and Philip.

"Go on—read them," urged Mr. Prendergast.
"Don't you take any notice of me; just you see what
that young man of yours has to say."

Anabelle put the letters into her bag.

"On board," she said. "I'll have lots of time to read
all the way home."

She was transhipped at the Clarksons', and lunch was served at once. There was a moment after the meal in which she found herself alone, with time to open Philip's letter. She glanced through it—once, swiftly; then she read it again; it should have been printed, she thought, and distributed to serve as a model of painstaking evasiveness. She put it into her bag, and with it put away from her mind any temptation to dwell on the implications of what he had not written. There would be time on board; time to think; four days in which to consider the situation.

Mr. Clarkson called to her; she went out and said goodbye to Mr. Prendergast; she thanked him warmly and sent affectionate messages to his family; then she took her place in Mr. Clarkson's car. Her luggage was already at the back. She was going. She was leaving Portugal. If she came back, it would be as Philip's wife.

If she came back . . .

One look at the *Yeoman,* alongside the dock in the port of Leixoes between a small Dutch vessel and a Swedish cargo boat, was sufficient to shatter the pleasant picture she had built up in her mind of a trim, gleaming white vessel, half liner, half yacht. The *Yeoman* was as sturdy as its name; it was low in the water, low in structure, and had lines strongly reminiscent of Noah's Ark. It was painted a gloomy shade of grey and looked uncompromisingly workaday. On the dock, a scattering of passengers were standing, and towards these Mr. Clarkson led her. The sight of him brought hearty cries of welcome.

"You've left it late, haven't you?" asked a florid, middle-aged man whose squat roundness was so like that of the *Yeoman* that Anabelle felt they might have been built as a pair. "Thought you weren't going to make it."

"Hello, Yule." Mr. Clarkson thumped him affectionately on the back. "No thinner, I see. Hello, Daisy, old girl."

Daisy-old-girl must be Mrs. Yule, decided Anabelle, content to await enlightenment until Mr. Clarkson had extricated himself from the confusion of greetings. Her glance round the dock and up at the two far-from-spacious decks on which more passengers were standing, showed her nobody near in age to herself. There were drooping moustaches, bald heads, wrinkles and whiskers and sagging chins; aggregate age, somewhere near a thousand, she calculated despondently.

But there was, she noted suddenly with relief, somebody young. A girl. Two girls. Like her, they appeared to view their fellow passengers with reserve; far from mingling, they stood at the railing staring out over the dock with frowning expressions.

She brought her attention back to Mr. Clarkson, who was presenting her to the woman he had addressed as Daisy.

"This is a good friend of mine, and I hope you'll look after her, Daisy," he said. "Her name's Anabelle. Anabelle Baird. Anabelle, this is Mrs. Yule. Mr. Yule, and Mr. and Mrs. Saville, Mr. and Mrs. Williams—ah! and here's our confirmed young bachelor, Hughie King. Hughie'll look after you—won't you, Hughie?"

Mr. King, kind old eyes beaming under shaggy white brows, quavered that he would be personally responsible for Miss Baird's welfare throughout the journey.

The *Yeoman* gave a sudden terrifying snort; Mrs. Yule gave a shriek and clutched her husband convulsively.

"All aboard, all aboard," shouted a jovial, red-faced man from the deck. "Come on, you loiterers. Coming aboard, Clarkson?"

Mr. Clarkson shook his head and shouted that he had to hurry away. He stood at the foot of the gangway shaking hands with his friends as they went up to the ship; as the last one passed him, he waved his farewells and, almost falling headlong in his efforts to walk forward and look backward for as long as the ship was in sight, disappeared from view. As he went, the preparations for putting to sea began.

"Now, we've got to look after you." Mrs. Yule, tiny and birdlike, looked up at Anabelle. "We're all good friends—"

"—and jolly good com-pan-ee," sang her husband. "You'll enjoy the trip, Miss Baird. Let's start off by calling you Anabelle, shall we? I'm known as Batty and my wife's Daisy. No formality here, as you'll find out."

"Come and meet everybody," urged Mrs. Yule. "You'll find . . . Why, *Beatrice!* I had no *idea* you were going to be on board!" She lowered her voice and drew nearer. "My dear, how did it go? Was it *too* awful?"

She drew Beatrice aside; a pity, Anabelle thought, that she would never know how awful. She found her hand grasped by a tall, thin, sharp-voiced woman.

"I'm Mrs. Grant—Mrs. Williams has just been telling me about you; how nice to have you aboard. I must introduce you to the Parker twins—such nice girls, both going to London for the Ogilvie wedding. You know the Ogilvies, of course? No? How extraordinary! I thought everybody knew the Ogilvies. I've known Clarissa—she's the one who's getting married —since she was *so* high. A church in Sloane Street— can't remember its name. They . . . Millie, stop a minute and come and meet Miss Baird. Incidentally, did you know that Kathy was on board?"

"Kathy! No! You're *sure?*"

"I've just been talking to her."

"Tell me, was she . . . I mean, was he . . . ?"

"No sign of him. I didn't like to ask."

"Well, Lorna'll know; I'll ask her. Oh, by the way, I just ran into Moira; she's unpacking—you know how she likes to get the entire collection hung up ready to wear. That makes two of us for bridge, and if Mary hasn't fixed up with the others, we can rope her in and . . . Oh, how about Miss Baird? Do you play bridge, Miss Baird?"

Anabelle said that she didn't, and it was immediately clear to her that she had seen the last of Mrs. Grant and Millie.

Left with the Parker twins, she found them totally uninterested in anything or anybody aboard; their attention was still directed ashore. They were very much alike; pretty, plump, with outfits that matched in every detail but that of colour.

The blue one, turning towards Anabelle, asked without notable interest whether she had been on one of Mr. Clarkson's ships before.

"No, I haven't."

"Well, it's pretty awful, but if you can get a decent group of younger people on board and stick to them, you're all right. This time"—she turned angrily to her sister—"we seem to have mucked it up. Ruth, you *couldn't* have told him properly."

Ruth swung round and snapped a reply.

"I tell you I *did*. I told him I'd seen Mr. Clarkson myself and that it was absolutely fixed."

"You're sure you sent him the ticket?"

"Of *course* I sent it! And he got it too because I went into the office and asked; they'd had a cheque in payment. So he *must* be coming, Mary."

"What's the use of coming if we're halfway across the Bay of Biscay? Look, they're going to pull up the gangway. And now we're both stuck on board without a decent man to talk to, or to dance with. I wish I'd—"

She broke off. There was a commotion on the quay. Turning to the rail, all three looked down.

A car had stopped so near the barrier that the wooden supports were still quivering from the impact. Three people were spilling out—a middle-aged couple and a younger man.

If Anabelle had had any instant of doubt, she would have found confirmation in the simultaneous shrieks of joy that were emitted by the Parker twins.

"*Angus!* How marvelous! Angus, *hurry!*"

He said a hurried farewell to his friends, grasped his hand luggage, leapt across the space that now intervened between ship and shore, and then reverted to his normal leisurely pace. He stepped on board to face, unmoved, all the passengers who had hurried to the side to find out the cause of the commotion. As his feet touched the deck, the twins possessed themselves of each of his arms—and that, Anabelle told herself, was the last she had seen of Mary and Ruth. And of Angus Pemberton too.

He raised a hand in friendly salute to her over the heads of the throng separating them. She returned it and then turned and walked away, leaving the chattering, all-good-friends atmosphere behind. Leaning over the rail, she wondered uneasily what she would find to do for the next four days. She had, she knew, no talent for merging into noisy groups. She would enjoy—very much enjoy—watching Millie and Beatrice and the rest, and it would be interesting to see which of the Parker twins won the contest for Angus Pemberton; but watching, even though amusing, could be a lonely business. She wished she had brought some books; she had no hope that the library on board, if library there were, would contain any very absorbing literature.

The ship was drawing away more swiftly from the shore. The figures on the dock were beginning to look like marionettes. Watching them, her eyes fell suddenly on a flutter of black at the end of the quay. A priest, his skirts wind-whipped.

She narrowed her eyes. It was too far to make out for certain, but . . . surely that was Father Vicento?

If the ship had been still alongside, nothing, she knew, could have prevented her from running down the gangway and . . . and what? She spoke no Portuguese, he no English. Even without the language barrier, there would have been nothing to say. He was alone; there was no old man, no friendly little boy. She might perhaps have learned whether the old man still lived, but after that, there would have been nothing to add. It would have been impossible to have asked him why Luis's grandfather had looked at her with a prayer in his eyes. How could Father Vicento have answered? He had been standing behind the wheel chair; the appeal, if appeal it had been, had been made in a brief moment, winged voicelessly from the old man to herself.

Quay and priest were fading from sight. There went Portugal and the Prendergasts. There went Philip and the Jansens. She thought of Philip's letter, thought of taking it out and reading it again, and then decided that she would keep her mind off problems. She would go down and unpack, only pausing to pray that Millie or Beatrice would not prove to be her cabin companion.

She turned towards the door that led below. Passing the still animated groups, she met friendly smiles, warm assurances that she was going to enjoy every minute of the trip; how nice to have her on board, and wait a minute, she hadn't met Tom and Essie Smith; wait till she heard Tom on his guitar; top-of-the-pops wasn't in it. Did she play mah-jong? Oh, pity; never mind; old Steve, poor old Steve, over there by the Yules, simply adored playing Scrabble and could never find anybody to play with him, so if she had any time . . .

The stairs were like stairs ashore—polished mahogany, with rubber treads down the center. The cabins —all were open as she passed—looked like illustrations in old issues of magazines like the *Strand;* no plastics, no space-saving fittings; they were less cabins than boudoirs, and she began to feel she was traveling on an out-of-date royal yacht. She wondered if the engine rooms were fitted out with the same happy disregard for modernity.

Where was Number Eight? No figures; gleaming little brass letters on every door. Two, Four, Six . . . this was it: Eight.

She was brought up on the point of entering by the emerging figure of a smiling, dark-skinned woman dressed in blue linen over which was a starched, snow-white apron; on her head was a frilled white cap.

"Miss Baird?" she asked.

Mees Bay-aird; Portuguese.

"Yes. Good evening."

"I am the maid for these cabins—my name is Maria. Any time you wish to call me, you must please ring your bell and I will come. For night it is Maria; daytime it is Odette. She too speaks English." She stood aside. "I hope you will be comfortable, and the little boy too."

Anabelle, on the threshold, paused.

"Little boy?"

"So good, so friendly, so happy. I have unpacked his clothes and I have put his empty suitcases under his bed," said Maria.

Anabelle was to wonder, much later, why she had had no premonition. Perhaps it was because her mind was filled with the buzz of arrival on board, where everybody knew everybody and where everybody began sentences and broke off in the middle to greet old friends. Jolly good com-pan-ee . . . all except Angus Pemberton, who had been plucked out of the throng by the Parker twins and who would share himself out generously between them on the voyage home. She had had no premonition; she had merely listened to Maria and had decided swiftly that she would rather be in a cabin with a small boy than with his too hearty parents—or grandparents.

Grandparents . . .

She had an instant's vision of the old man, and of Father Vicento on the quay. She thought of the small, dark, vivid face of Luis Antonio Jose Ribeiro—and so it was no wonder that when she heard a rush of footsteps down the corridor, when she felt her hand seized, when she looked down and saw the small, dark, vivid face, she had the feeling of being in a dream.

His words were prosaic enough.

"You were late! You were so late! I thought already that you would lose the ship! I looked here in the cabin, and there was no baggage, and—"

"He was so worried," smiled Maria. "I thought he would begin to cry."

"Not cry," denied Luis. "Worried—yes, I was worried."

"I took him up to the bridge, so that he could look out for you."

"But up there, they showed me the big wheel, and so I did not see you when you came," explained Luis. "Then when the ship began to go, I had to wave my hand to Father Vicento—"

"So it *was* Father Vicento."

"He brought me."

"He came on board, but not for long," Maria said. "Only to see, to arrange some of Luis's luggage, to tell me about what he likes to eat. Then he had to go."

"But he said that he would wait to see you come," Luis said.

Anabelle's head was clearer.

"Are you traveling alone?" she asked him.

"With you, of course," he corrected. "My grandfather said that when he is better, I can come back—if I wish to come back."

Was that the appeal? Was she to look after Luis on the journey to England? It seemed a small thing to ask; perhaps he had simply wanted to ask her to accept the passage on the *Yeoman* if it was offered to her.

"Now Luis will be happy," Maria said. "If you want anything, please to ring."

She went away, large and full-bosomed and motherly. Anabelle walked into the cabin and looked round.

Not cramped; comfortable. More mahogany, two beds with wooden sides, a thick carpet, frilled muslin curtains over the porthole, a bathroom with a small zinc bath beside the large porcelain one—for fresh water, Luis explained; to take off the soap.

She unpacked enough for the journey, noting uneasily that the ship was beginning to roll slightly.

"Are you a good sailor?" she asked Luis.

"Please?"

"Do you think you'll feel . . . ?" Well, what was the use of putting ideas into his head? If he was sick, he was sick, and she would have to look after him—if she wasn't sick too.

"Is this your first time on a ship?" she asked.

"First time?" He sounded surprised. "No, not first time. My grandfather had a little ship, a—"

"A yacht?"

"A little ship. He used to take me with him, or send me with Manuel and the other. We used to catch fish —big, big fish."

His arms were spread wide. The typical fisherman's attitude, she reflected, smiling to herself and putting him gently aside as she bent to push her suitcases under her bed. All fitted but one; perhaps she could put that on Luis's side; yes, there was room.

She put the last case beside his neatly aligned ones. She had straightened, she had even begun to arrange her dresses in the solid, gleaming wardrobe when the significance of what she had just seen came to her.

She turned. Stooping, remaining for a few moments crouched before his suitcases staring . . . she confirmed what she already knew, what she had already seen without seeing. His labels—every label on every case—had been neatly inscribed with his name and . . .

And with her address.

There was no mistake. All read alike: Luis Antonio Jose Ribeiro. The Coach House. Steyne. Hampshire. England.

Not even care of . . .

She looked down at him. He looked as serene, as confident, as secure in her protection as James and John had done. She spoke as casually as she could.

"Luis, who brought you to the ship?"

He was experimenting with the bathroom door—a sliding one.

"Father Vicento brought me."

"Nobody else?"

"My grandfather wished to come, but he did not feel strong."

"Did he . . . did your grandfather give you a letter for me?"

He spread his hands, raised his shoulders and so had no need to reply; the answer was in the negative.

"Where will you stay when you're in England, Luis?"

He turned from the door, astonished. He bent to the labels, spelling them out slowly.

"The Coach House, Steyne, Hampshire, England. That is the name of your house, no? Father Vicento did not make a mistake?"

"Did he write the labels?"

"Yes—but my grandfather told him the names."

"How . . . how long are you going to stay in England?"

He put a hand in hers and pulled her towards the door of the cabin; there was much to be seen up on deck.

"We can talk upstairs, no?"

Keeping his hand in hers, she sat down on the side of her bed.

"I'll go up on deck with you presently," she said.

"Please, that word?"

"Presently; in a little while. First tell me how long you're going to stay in England."

"When my grandfather is better, he will send for me."

"And . . . and until then?"

He smiled—a smile full of confidence and growing affection.

"Until he is better, I shall stay with you."

Until he is better . . .

She had a sudden need for air even more urgent than Luis's. But as she reached the door, Maria appeared, a printed menu in hand.

"I am glad to catch you before you leave the cabin," she said. "Otherwise I should look all over the decks and in the lounge." She held out the menu. "This is to choose from," she explained. "The steward will come presently to say when it is ready—dinner for the *menino*." She looked down smilingly at Luis. "You see, there are no other little *meninos* or *meninas* on the ship this time; you are the only one, so poor you, you will have to eat with only yourself."

"Miss Baird will come too," he stated positively. He brushed aside the menu. "I do not care what," he said, "and it is too early to eat my dinner; at home, I had it with my grandfather, late, and then I went to bed."

"They won't let you have meals with the grown-ups," Maria said. "But Miss Baird can go and sit with you if you like."

Anabelle, her mind on other matters, absently chose a light meal. Then she addressed Maria impulsively.

"Will you take Luis up on deck for a few moments, please? Or keep him with you; I'll go to the dining room in ten minutes and wait for him there."

Luis clutched at her dress as she was leaving.

"You will come back soon?"

He was not alarmed—but he was on the verge of alarm. A sudden realization of his situation swept over her and left her feeling weak. He knew nothing beyond the fact that he was in her care. He had not learned to mistrust—yet. There was a cloud drifting across his blue Portuguese skies, but it had not yet overshadowed him.

She spoke firmly.

"Dining room in ten minutes from now," she said. "I promise."

Even a child could recognize the sincerity of the last two words. Luis, satisfied, released her.

She had no idea, at first, where she was going. She had to talk to somebody. She had to find out if any messages had been left for her, any letters, any word. The purser would know.

The boy, she was told, had come aboard with a priest. No, there was no message.

She managed to maintain an outward calm. It would not do to run agitatedly round the ship stating that there was a boy in her cabin who expected to be taken to her home indefinitely. She thought of going to the captain, but the facts were so sparse, and what facts there were so lacking in credibility, that she came to a despairing halt.

Panic gripped her. She could look after the boy, and she knew that her father would raise no objections to his staying at Steyne—but there was something behind the situation that frightened her.

Round her, as she reached the deck, were the all-good-friends. She was claimed at once by Mrs. Yule and asked to go to the bar for a drink. Refusing as politely as she could, she evaded two more sociable groups—and then halted. Before her, once more leaning negligently over a rail, she saw the one person to whom she could tell her story. Angus Pemberton. He knew her; he knew her background and her history and her family; he was the only one on board the

Yeoman who would listen without coming to the conclusion that she was hysterical.

One of the twins—the green one—was beside him; there was, Anabelle noted without resentment, no friendly invitation from either to join them. Intrusion was the last thing she would in normal circumstances have dreamed of, but necessity was driving her.

As she hesitated, the white-haired old man known as "our bachelor" endeared himself to her for ever by appearing on deck and hailing Angus's companion. Going up to her, he took her arm and insisted on her joining the large party on its way to the bar.

"Won't take no for an answer," he stated obstinately. "Whole gang of us going to drink to the trip: Oporto Unlimited. Just one little drink, and then you can come back and get on with your flirting. Come along. You too, Pemberton. And how about you, Miss Baird, or may I say Anabelle?"

"Thank you. I'll . . . I'll come in just a minute. I wanted to say a word to Mr. Pemberton."

Angus had turned; now it was his back that was against the rail. He looked amused as his companion, scowling, was urged relentlessly towards the lounge.

"I won't keep you long," Anabelle told him.

He looked at her.

"What's the hurry? You and I aren't members of Oporto Unlimited."

She saw that they were alone on the deck. The sea was calm, but the ship had fallen into the slow, relentless roll that was to continue throughout the journey. Beyond the heavy doors, the jolly good company could be heard singing in the bar. Somebody began to strum a piano. A Portuguese steward appeared, tidied the deck, and hurried inside again.

Angus's eyes were on her; he was waiting for her to speak.

"You look pale," he commented at last. "Feeling the motion?"

His ease, his obvious freedom from anxiety of any kind, gave her a sudden helpless feeling of rage. Sleek, like a tomcat, she thought furiously; no problems, no responsibilities. She wished ardently that he would fall overboard, leaving Keith in his place. Keith could have dealt with this.

"Something's happened," she began abruptly and then stopped, unable to go on.

He frowned, but his voice was calm.

"Man overboard?"

"I'm in a two-berth cabin. The other person in it is a five-year-old boy and . . . and all his luggage labels have got my address on them."

He considered.

"Your address? Steyne address?"

"Yes. Clearly written in full: The Coach House, Steyne, Hampshire, England."

There was a pause. He had straightened, but that was all; none of her tension seemed to have communicated itself to him.

"Go on," he invited.

"But . . . but that's all." There was a note of desperation in her voice. "There isn't any more. He's just *there*. A priest brought him on board, and there's no message of any kind for me—I've just been asking."

"You mean a little boy you never saw before is—"

"I saw him once. Do you remember the fair we went to with the Prendergasts?"

"At Virgilio?"

"Yes. He was there, with an old man—"

"I remember. This is your old man in the wheel chair?"

"Yes. I saw the same priest on the quay just after the ship sailed—I couldn't have sworn it was Father Vicento, but it must have been, because it was he who brought Luis aboard."

"Luis?"

"The boy. What can I do?"

"Do?"

"Yes, *do*. I've got to do something, haven't I? I can't just accept a small boy like a . . . like a parcel."

"Well, all one can say is"—he spoke judicially— "that you've got him. There's no longer any question of accepting or rejecting; your problem is how to get rid of him."

"Rid of him?"

His eyebrows went up; she saw bewilderment in his glance.

"Let's recap," he said patiently. "I take it you came to me because your story, told to anybody else, might have raised questions as to your stability—right?"

"Stability?" She let it go. "Yes. But—"

"Knowing you, I can believe what you say—so without more delay, we can proceed to the next phase. You've got him; you didn't ask for him; you don't want him. Correct?"

"Yes."

He studied her.

"Perhaps we're going too fast," he suggested. "*Did* you, in any sense of the word, ask for him? Cast your mind back and remember that you're dealing with Portuguese—people you don't know the first thing about. Try to remember whether, at that fair, you did anything, said anything that might have been taken to—"

"The boy—Luis—joined us. Then Clare came up and the boy went back to his grandfather and said that the old man would like to speak to me."

"And he said?"

"He thanked me. I asked him when Luis was going to England."

"Luis had told you that?"

"Yes. His grandfather said that he was going soon, but there were difficulties. Opposition was the word he used. He asked me when I was going to be married, and it was then, I think, that I noticed how ill he was. There wasn't any . . . any outward struggle, but he could hardly breathe."

"In other words, what he was saying may not have sounded important to you but was obviously so to him. Go on."

His voice was suddenly authoritative, and a sense of relief came to her; he had at least decided against total detachment.

"He said he had wanted to see me and speak to me. He said he was now satisfied. He said there wasn't much time to talk—and when he said it, I knew he meant that he was dying. The only thing—"

"Well?"

"He knew my name. I suppose I should have asked him at once *how* he knew it, but all I was thinking of at the time was his helplessness and . . . If you're faced with a man who conveys to you quite clearly that he's dying, you—"

"Your feelings take over from your judgment. So we come back to the crucial question: how do you return this parcel of little boy?"

"Well, how?"

He paused to consider; then he spoke in the same firm voice.

"The captain," he said. "Go to him and tell him the facts; if he wants corroboration, he can send for me. He'll get in touch with the agents and find out who arranged the boy's passage. Speaking of passages, why not look on his ticket and find out—"

"I looked. He's traveling on a . . ."

"On a—?"

"It isn't a return ticket. It's a single."

"Well, single or return, the agents must know who applied for it and who paid for it. They'll get in touch with the police and—"

"*Police!*"

"Police. Who else? People can't park small boys on a ship with just a couple of labels to . . . You're sure there was no message?"

"Quite sure. What sort of message could there have been, anyhow?"

"Quite so; the facts speak for themselves. Well, you don't have to worry. My own bet is that the ship will turn back. We're not far out from Leixoes, we're not a mail ship, and we don't, as far as I can see, run on a tight schedule. The matter boils down to the ordinary stowaway pattern; we'll turn back and the police will come out on a launch and take the boy off; after that, it'll be their business to—"

"*No.*"

He stopped and looked at her. She had spoken in a low, choked voice. Her face was very pale; one hand was gripping the rail.

"You came to me," he pointed out, "for advice. I'm giving it to you."

"What has *he* done?" she broke out fiercely.

"He?"

"The boy. Luis. Captain, agents, police . . . *police!* What has he *done?* Nothing—except believe that he's going to England. He's down there now, waiting for me, feeling *how?* How would you feel if you were dumped on a total stranger going to a strange land? Inside, I mean. Outwardly he's . . ."

For some moments she was unable to go on. She saw in Angus's eyes nothing but a calm, steady patience.

"No," she said. "Thank you for trying to help, but I won't do it. I'm sorry I bothered you."

She very much regretted her impulsive appeal—it had been, she knew now, for sympathy and not for advice. She wished she had waited until her panic had subsided and she had been able to think over the matter coolly—but she realized, with a kind of grudging gratitude, that Angus Pemberton's academic, unemotional attitude to the problem had supplied the astringent touch necessary to force her to make her own decision.

"My time," he said, "is all yours. If you'd like me—"

"Thank you, no. I'm grateful to you for listening."

"I was going to say that if you want me to go to the captain with you, I will."

She spoke in a composed and level voice.

"I'm not going to the captain," she said. "I'm not going to anybody."

"Then—?"

"I'm going to do what's best for the boy. Somewhere, under his confidence, there's a feeling that . . . He's frightened. He doesn't know he's frightened, but if I say or do anything to confirm what he knows already—namely, that his well-being is resting solely on me—and who, after all, am I in his life?—then he'll panic. If he knows that the ship is turning back, that he's got to be taken off by uniformed police . . . No. No and no and no."

"You're not"—he seemed to choose his words—"you're not frightened of being caught up in anything—"

"Political? That's what Keith said."

"I was merely going to say that you ought to do a bit more thinking; you may be swimming into deep waters."

"I liked the old man. I liked the priest. The boy is . . . he's a beautiful little boy. He's arrogant, and by English standards spoilt; I've no idea how he'll get on with me—but for the moment, I'm going to look at it from his point of view and not from any other. I'm pretty sure that when we get home, somebody'll turn up with instructions, or I'll find out where he's to go. But I don't see any reason to have him thrown off the ship. I'm sorry I lost my head. I'll be grateful if you'll keep all this to yourself."

She left him and went straight to the dining saloon. If she had needed any confirmation of her own convictions, it was there, in the desolate look of the child's figure standing in the doorway awaiting her. The sudden radiance in his face, the eager clutch at her hand, the gradual return of the look of confidence to his eyes—these were enough to arouse in her a hard determination to give him what protection she could.

Something was going on—something that would, that must be cleared up in the near future. Guessing was useless. An old man was dying and for some reason of his own wanted her to look after his grandchild. Well, she would do just that.

Luis was looking up at her.

"I'm not hungry," he said.

"Well, *I'm* starving."

"You are"—eagerness crept into his voice—"you are going to eat with me?"

"I certainly am."

"But your dinner is later."

"I'll fix it so's I can have it with you. I'd rather," she said with a patent sincerity that made him give a sudden skip of joy. "I'd much rather have dinner with you than with all those other people. I don't know any of them. I'd rather stay with someone I know— like you."

He needed only one further reassurance. Seated opposite her at a corner table for two, he put a not too anxious query.

"You like that I am going to stay in your house in England?"

She smiled at him. It was a smile as warm and as comforting as an embrace.

"I like," she said.

Chapter Four

BY THE TIME the *Yeoman* had settled against her berth in a London dock, Anabelle felt that she knew as much about Luis as anybody could know of the workings of a little boy's mind. She had learned something of his tastes and of his interests; she knew that he disliked eggs and could not be induced to drink milk. He chose his clothes with care, from a wardrobe that could only be termed extensive; he liked to be neat, he loathed being dirty. He was uninterested in drawing or in painting or in crayons; he cared nothing for the toys Maria offered him from the ship's stock.

He could read and, with some assistance, form letters and figures, but books did not interest him unless they were read aloud. He required no assistance in dressing or undressing; all that was needed was somebody to pick up the things he left on the floor. He disliked walking but claimed to be able to swim, ride, and jump a pony through hoops.

He was happiest in adult company; left alone, even though surrounded by the normal distractions of childhood, he sat idle, expectant, until his solitude was relieved. In company he sat quiet and attentive, making none of the demands usual in children for attention to questions or complaints. He would have answered Mrs. Yule's description of him as a little old

man if it had not been for the fact that he had a
childish sense of fun that overcame him at unexpected
moments and sent him into fits of mirth, smothered in
the nearest pillow or cushion. At such times Anabelle
loved him most—but at all times, she realized in dismay long before they reached England, he had come
to mean much to her. He was like no other small boy
she had ever met—and he seemed peculiarly her own.

Her guardianship had raised no comment on the
ship; she was understood to be in charge of him; he
was going to stay for a time at her home. He was uni-
versally liked, but nobody showed any unusual interest in him; nobody probed.

Angus Pemberton was the only person on board
with whom he talked Portuguese. Most of the passengers had been long enough in Portugal to be familiar
with the language, but it was only Angus, speaking
fluently but with Brazilian overtones that amused Luis
very much, who refused to address him in English.
Between the two was an easy comradeship that irri-
tated the Parker twins very much, for though in many
ways precocious, Luis had still to learn when it would
be tactful to withdraw. So much time, indeed, did he
spend with Angus that Anabelle found herself wondering how much of Luis's background had emerged
during their talks. She would have liked to ask, but
detaching Angus from the twins was all but impossible. Then one day towards the end of the voyage, he
detached himself effortlessly and sought her out—but
not to fill in gaps in her knowledge of Luis; he
wanted only to put before her some of the difficulties
of her situation.

"I've been thinking; he's an alien, so every so
often—"

"I know," she said. "Report to the police. I know
all about alien regulations; I went through it all in the
past when your grandmother had foreign maids. I'll
take him and report whenever I have to—and in case
you were going to bring it up, I'll also see that he
goes to Mass on Sundays. What I'm more interested
in is whether you've found out any more about him?"

"You don't find out much from little boys of five.

It's horse work just trying to make them stick to facts. One or two things did emerge."

"Such as what?"

"He says that his grandmother died on his fifth birthday—that is, two and a half months ago."

"And his parents?"

"He asserts positively that he never had any."

"That's what he told me."

"Father Vicento was the family priest."

"I knew that already. He taught Luis too; taught him very well. Didn't you find out anything else?"

"If you'd told me you wanted me to prepare a dossier, I would have taken more pains," he said coldly.

"You've spent hours and hours with him; he must have talked about *something*. Did he play with other children? Were there any other children? Is he the only grandchild?"

"Apparently. He didn't mention any children—beyond the children of the staff; the setup was pretty elaborate, as perhaps you've gathered. Which is what makes me certain that even if there's no message for you in England, there'll be money."

"Money?"

"Or perhaps not," he amended. "Whoever took a chance on you, showed a confidence that might turn out to extend to matters of finance too."

"Didn't he talk about any other relations?"

"Only one, and I didn't press it, because he shied away. There was an uncle Alfredo, who seems to have turned up at intervals and cast a blight."

"He didn't live with Luis and his grandparents?"

"No. Luis doesn't know where he came from, but he was always glad to see him go. There was some talk, it seemed, of Uncle Alfredo wanting Luis to go and live with him. Luis didn't like the idea at all; his grandfather seems to have liked it even less. Uncle Alfredo's visits left them all feeling upset."

"Could he—this Uncle Alfredo—have been the opposition that Luis's grandfather mentioned when he was talking to me?"

"If he wanted Luis to live with him, and Luis's grandfather wanted the boy to go to England, then you might say that uncle was some kind of stumbling block—but it's only guesswork. Luis disliked him; he says he was fat. Very fat. That's the only description he offered." He looked at Anabelle curiously. "What," he asked, "is your father going to say to all this?"

She opened her mouth to reply and instead began to laugh. After some moments, Angus laughed too.

"Well, yes; I see what you mean," he said. "He won't say anything. I'd forgotten that talent of his for minding his own business."

"I sent him a cable asking him to meet the ship."

"That was wise. Perhaps there'll be somebody standing on the quay waiting to claim Luis."

Nobody claimed Luis, but when her father came aboard, Anabelle told her story—briefly, without comment, but putting in every fact as she knew it. He listened in silence; at the end, he took off his glasses, polished them, and put them on again.

"Ah," he said. "Yes . . . well. Dear me."

It was as much as she had expected; it sufficed. She had put a coin into the machine; the works were in motion. A human computer—but one that was reluctant to give out its conclusions.

They went ashore with Luis; the landing formalities completed, they put their luggage aboard the roomy, old-fashioned car that had served Mr. Baird for the past twenty-five years.

"This automobile," Luis said, surveying it in surprise, "is very strange." His eyes rested on Mr. Baird; it was clear that only his customary politeness prevented him from saying that Mr. Baird was stranger still.

He was nearing sixty, tall, thin, and stooping, with a curiously boneless look. His face, studious, bespectacled, could never have been handsome; his hair, thin to vanishing point, sprouted from his scalp in a manner reminiscent of palm fronds.

His wife had died suddenly; Anabelle had been twelve, Clare eleven, and Olivia five. A meeting of his sisters, hastily convened, resulted in one of them being sent down to Steyne—to cope, she told her brother on her arrival. Mr. Baird greeted her absently and went on hanging up the washing. The house was spotless, the midday meal was cooking. The two elder girls were away at boarding school; Olivia was playing happily in the garden. Listening to his sister's plan to take over until she had found and installed a good housekeeper, Mr. Baird showed her a room already prepared for her reception, served lunch, fed Olivia, donned an apron and did the washing up, ironed the clothes, peeled vegetables for the evening meal, mowed the lawn, made tea, cooked a light dinner, and put Olivia to bed. At the end of three days, during which his sole comment on her plans for his future, and that of his daughters, had been "Ah," she left. On her departure, Mr. Baird added a neatly written notice to those pinned up outside the tobacconist's window, and selected from three applicants a daily woman who cleaned the house and did the washing and ironing; he himself continued to cook until his daughters grew old enough to relieve him of the task. As well as cooking, he revised the series of textbooks entitled *Baird's Full Course in Arithmetic;* he also translated obscure works into Italian, wrote papers on the subject of pests in vegetable gardens, and played the flute. His children had never heard him voice an opinion until asked for one, and not always then; his attitude had at one time seemed to them less than paternal, but from wondering whether he should have exerted more authority they had ended with the conviction that he was all a parent should be.

Baird's Course brought in a moderate income until the evening on which a well-known professor mentioned it—quite without meaning to, he explained apologetically afterwards—during a talk on television. Thereafter the series had become standard textbooks in a greatly increased number of schools throughout the country, and the royalties would have enabled the author to sell the Coach House and buy something a good deal bigger—but the Bairds had not moved. It was to the Coach House that Mr. Baird and Anabelle and Luis were about to drive now.

Mr. Baird was at the wheel. He was a nervous

driver, but as his fears at driving were nothing to his terrors at being driven, his passengers endured as best they might.

"Car keys," he said, fumbling in his pockets. "I'm sure I brought them. Yes, here they are. Move over, will you, Anabelle? I like to have the gears clear. Is the boy all right at the back?"

"Yes, he is."

"Then we may as well get along."

They got along. Passing a vehicle was a rare occurrence; nothing went more slowly than the Baird car with Mr. Baird at the wheel. Getting past was a harrowing business for everybody.

"The car is big, but it does not go fast," Luis pointed out unnecessarily.

"There's no hurry, you know," Mr. Baird explained. "We've plenty of time; no need to rush."

"I think you could pass that cart," Anabelle told him when they had followed it for several miles. "If you'll pull out a bit, I'll tell you if anything's coming."

"Perhaps he'll turn off in a minute or two; they often do."

"You can't keep behind a farm cart all the way home, Father. Pull out a bit. A bit more."

"My dear, I'm in the middle of the road and—look out! Something coming."

"It was miles away; you could have got by quite easily."

"I wish that fellow behind us wouldn't edge up so close. Sit down, will you, Luis? I like to keep the rear window clear."

They stopped to buy food; from now on, Anabelle remembered, it would be new ground for Luis; he was to have his first glimpse of a world in which people, for the most part, fended for themselves. Round-eyed, he watched her choosing meat and buying tin stores and fruit. On reaching the house, he inspected it from floor to attic, his expression more and more amazed.

"Where," he enquired at last of Anabelle, "do your servants live?"

"She lives in her own house," Anabelle explained. "She comes every morning at nine and goes back to her own home again at half-past twelve."

"She? You have only one?"

"You wouldn't really call it one," she confided. "Let's say half a one; she's old, and rather slow, and we don't push her; what she can do, she does. What she does, she does well."

"You have"—he paused delicately—"no other cars?"

"Not one."

"No . . . no horses?"

"If you want to ride, you've only to say the word; there's a farmer who lets out horses at so much an hour."

"That land with the trees—it is yours?"

"The wood? No. It belongs to Angus's mother. You know that he lives next door; the wall divides our garden from his, but all the woods round this house and their house belong to Angus's grandmother, Lady Evelyn Pemberton. This house is called the Coach House because the Pemberton coaches were once kept here. But nowadays no more coaches."

His eyes were on the distant view of the sea.

"You have a boat?"

"Well, we had a dinghy once, but Clare went sailing and didn't tie it up properly, and that night there was a storm, and the next day . . ."

"No ding-hy?"

"No dinghy. But if you want to sail, let me know; we know someone who used to be in the navy, and he owns a nice little boat and takes us out whenever we want to go. Weather, of course, permitting."

"And you yourself, you do the cooking?"

"I myself. Do you want to shell peas, or would you rather go outside and look round?"

With the delicacy that came so naturally to him, he explained, without explaining, that shelling peas was not on his programme. He passed Mr. Baird in the doorway, and for some moments the man stood staring thoughtfully after the boy.

"Looks like a Velásquez," he said. "I can't make up my mind which one. He calls Angus Angus,"

"And me Anabelle; if he was going to be around for some time, it seemed silly to be formal."

"I see."

"Do you like him?"

"Luis? He seems a nice little boy. Did I say Velásquez?"

"You did."

He seemed to have nothing more to say. He was on his way upstairs when Anabelle called him.

"Mr. Baird."

They had tried, when young, to draw his attention from his work. Toiling up to his study at the top of the house, they had said in turn Father, Daddy, Dad, I say, Look here, Hey you—and at last, in desperation, Mr. Baird. To this last he had at once responded. Mr. Baird he had remained when there were matters of import to be discussed.

"Could you," she asked, "sit down and talk to me for a few minutes?"

"Of course, my dear. You wouldn't rather go upstairs to my study?"

"That's your workroom; this is mine."

He sat down on the stool she placed for him and put his arms on the kitchen table—a quiet, shy man with mild blue eyes—eyes, Anabelle knew, that saw more than they seemed to see.

"I suppose it's about Luis," he said. "It's a difficult situation."

"Angus Pemberton said I might be getting into deep water."

"It's quite possible, my dear."

"I told you all the facts and you've had time to think over them. Did I do right in deciding to keep him?"

He looked at her in surprise.

"You had no choice," he pointed out. "I mean to say that you, *being* you, would never for a moment have thought of doing anything else. That's what he saw at once, of course."

"That's what who saw?"

"The poor old grandfather you mentioned. Seeing you with James and John, he'd know at once that any child would be safe in your care. One sees it clearly whenever you're with children—sees it in you and misses it in Clare. Was that all you wanted to discuss with me?"

"No; that was only the first item on the agenda. There are others."

"Ah, your fiancé, of course. I'm sorry I haven't asked you about him, but your arrival with Luis put it out of my head. Is he back in Lisbon?"

"I don't know and at this moment I don't care. I want to ask you one or two things about Angus Pemberton. Now that he's back, I'd like to clear up one or two facts. You don't get facts out of Lady Evelyn; you only get opinions, and pretty biased ones at that. Why exactly did he go away?"

"My dear, you know quite well why he went away. He never got on with his grandmother—and it isn't to be wondered at. She's a very silly old woman, though perhaps I oughtn't to say so to you."

"Was there any specific quarrel at the end?"

"No. You could call it, I suppose, the culmination. She never knew how to handle him. It's a pity she had none of that maternal strain we were talking about just now in connection with yourself."

"When did Angus's parents die?"

"He was six or seven. A bad age at which to lose both parents."

"He had a tutor once. Thinking about it on board, I wondered . . . why couldn't it have been you?"

"Me? I would have been the last, the very last man Lady Evelyn would have appointed."

"Why?"

"Didn't she ever mention it?"

"Never, and neither did you. How about mentioning it now?"

He pulled out his underlip broodingly.

"It's a long, long time ago; it's all over and done with; all forgotten."

"Chapter one, para one," she said relentlessly.

"Well, it's easily told. Lady Evelyn had only one

child—a son. Like a great many mothers, she set her heart on his marrying a woman—a beautiful young woman—of her own choice. She threw them together in London, and then she invited her down here to Steyne. But the young woman didn't fall in with the plan. She married someone else."

"Who else?"

"Eh?"

"You heard me perfectly well. She married you, didn't she?"

"Yes. She did."

They stared at one another, and there was astonishment on both faces. Mr. Baird was not seeing his daughter; he was looking at a girl not unlike her, who had turned away from a man well endowed physically and financially to marry a penniless schoolmaster. Anabelle was wondering how her mother could possibly have seen below the unpromising surface to the treasure that lay below.

"You're wondering what she saw in me. I shall never know," Mr. Baird said slowly. "Neither, of course, will Lady Evelyn."

"You were teaching then?"

"I was mathematics master at St. Thomas's College. Lady Evelyn was chairman of the board and liked to bring visitors over. While she was at tea with the governors, I was asked to take your mother round the grounds. I don't remember doing so. I saw more of her, of course; I was at that time negotiating for the purchase of this house and was often at the big house discussing the matter. I brought your mother over here to look at Coach House, and we went back, I remember, to tell Lady Evelyn that we were engaged."

"And Lady Evelyn—?"

"She doesn't bear up well under disappointments. The immediate result was my dismissal from the school. It was a good thing, because I had had in mind for some time this series of textbooks. The dismissal offered, as your mother pointed out, an opportunity to write them. So I wrote them."

"When did Lady Evelyn forgive you?"

"She consented to be your godmother; perhaps it was then. She may have forgiven, but she didn't forget, and that was a pity, because I think I could have been of use to Angus on many occasions in his youth —if I had been allowed. He didn't have a very easy time."

"I suppose she told you he was coming home?"

"She got a letter from him just after you left for Portugal. She brought it over and showed it to me."

"Was she pleased?"

"Very far from pleased."

"But she must have been surprised."

"If she was, I wasn't," said Mr. Baird.

Anabelle stared at him.

"Why weren't you? Did you know he was coming?"

"There were reasons why I felt he would have to come."

"What reasons?"

He hesitated.

"It's a confidential matter, but it strikes me that you may know more about it than I do. That is, you probably know that a month or so ago Lady Evelyn changed her lawyers."

"I didn't know a thing."

"She didn't mention it?"

"Not a word."

"Having access to her papers, I thought you would have—"

"I never see any of the legal papers. Do you mean she's quarreled with old Mr. Sanders?"

"Yes. She told him—and he told me—that she no longer required his services."

Anabelle thought it over.

"I see. She wanted to do something—something about her money—that he didn't agree to. Is that it?"

"My dear, even if Sanders had told me, I couldn't tell you."

"No," she admitted, "I suppose you couldn't. But you think that's why Angus Pemberton has come home?"

"I think it more than likely."

"He told us at the Prendergasts' that that was his reason, but we thought he was fooling."

"It's a very wise move."

"To go off for ever, and then come running back because he thinks his inheritance is threatened—wise?"

"Very wise."

"How much can she deprive him of? Isn't there anything in trust?"

"Nothing was left in trust. Until Angus is thirty, she has full control."

"And when he's thirty?"

"He gets the capital; she gets a yearly income."

"He'll be thirty"—she worked it out—"in two weeks."

"Quite so."

"But what does he think his coming home can do? They never got on; they always got on each other's nerves, and they always will. Staying away, I would have thought he had a better chance of making headway with her than coming back like this."

"I didn't see him on the *Yeoman* when I went to meet you, so I can't judge whether he has changed or not. Seven years can do a lot for a man, especially when he has a basis of sound sense, as Angus always had. His misfortune was that he didn't get away from his grandmother much earlier. . . . And now, my dear, I have work to do."

He rose.

"There's the last item on the agenda," she said. "Philip."

Still seated at the table, her elbow on the smooth plastic surface, her head resting on her hand, she appeared lost in thought. Mr. Baird did not hurry her.

"When I told you I was engaged to him," she asked, "were you pleased?"

"I certainly wasn't surprised; you spent a good deal of time with him and seemed interested in nobody else."

"Were you pleased?"

"At twenty-five, I felt, you must know what you wanted. He had a difficult childhood."

"Were you pleased?"

"His mother—"

"Were you pleased?"

Mr. Baird pushed his glasses high on his forehead, peering down at her with a distressed frown.

"My dear . . ."

"Or didn't you care one way or the other?"

"I have never," he said slowly, as though groping for words, "felt myself able to judge how others should act."

"Not even your daughters?"

"Least of all my daughters. I have always tried to offer a solution to your difficulties, if a solution could be found; but to presume to say whether this or that young man would be a suitable life partner for you . . . no."

"Philip arrived at the Prendergasts' with a suggestion of putting off our wedding until Mr. Jansen's Rome office was opened."

"You gave him, I suppose, an answer of some kind?"

"He's reconsidering—or Mr. Jansen's reconsidering. I don't like the Jansens and I don't like Philip's servile attitude towards them. I got a letter from him just before I left Portugal; he said exactly nothing. He skated gracefully round the crisis."

"Is it a crisis?"

"I think so. I feel as though I'm so delicately balanced that a show of strength from Philip could send me one way and a show of dislike from you could send me the other."

"Then perhaps it really is a crisis," agreed Mr. Baird, "and Philip himself will tip the balance; in your present state of mind, there will not be the slightest need of any outside interference."

He settled his glasses on his nose and gazed at her for a few moments in silence. Then his eyes went to the stove. He sniffed anxiously.

"Anabelle . . ."

She rose and adjusted the heat. She opened the oven and glanced at the meat; when she looked up, she was alone. Luis's footsteps were sounding on the flagged path outside.

"Your father has gone?" he asked as he entered.

"He'll be down for lunch. After lunch you can come with me to meet Angus's grandmother."

"She also is Evelyn?"

"She also. She's my godmother and I was named after her. I'm John Evelyn Trevor's godmother and *he* was named after *me*. See?"

"Yes. Thank you. I think that Angus has come home. I saw a car like the car he said he was going to have."

"Then you'll probably see him too."

Approaching the large, beautiful, ivy-covered house after lunch had been cleared away and a reasonable interval allowed for Lady Evelyn's nap, she felt that Luis was going to present some difficulty; she could not leave him with her father, and she could not have him with her while she was at work. School was a solution, but it was impossible to guess how long he was going to be at Steyne. Putting the matter out of her mind, she waited for his comments as they came out of the woods onto the wide, beech-shaded avenue and the lovely building came in sight.

But one building was the same as another to Luis; he was interested only in learning something more of Lady Evelyn.

"You work for her?"

"Yes. She has a kind of shop—a special shop; people bring things and we sell them and all the money goes to charity."

"Charity? The poor people?"

"Yes. While I'm working, you can amuse yourself in the garden—as you see, there's quite a spread, so don't get lost."

"I would rather stay with you."

She was about to explain the difficulties of this when she heard the sound of horse's hoofs. Moments later, Angus Pemberton rode into view. She stepped to the edge of the drive; she liked horses and could manage the poorer spirited of the species, but she had never been able to disregard their prancing hoofs and freely displayed teeth as Luis was doing now. His delight at seeing both Angus and the horse was evident.

"You have more horses?" he shouted eagerly. "I shall ride?"

"Give me time," Angus said. "I'm trying this one out."

"You will buy it?"

"Not this one; he hasn't been taught good manners. I'm taking him back. If you come with me, we might see if there's a pony you can ride—if you can ride."

Luis, by way of answer, put out a hand; the next moment he was seated on the saddle in front of Angus, gathering up the reins in an expert manner. He looked eager and fearless.

"How about you?" Angus asked Anabelle. "Why not give yourself a day off and come too?"

"If you wouldn't mind taking Luis . . ."

He laughed.

"Luis, she wants me to take charge of you while she's at work. She brings you to England and takes the first chance of throwing you out to be looked after by somebody else." He looked down at Anabelle. "I inspected the shop," he said. "My grandmother said she'd let it get rather untidy; in other words, it's one big mess. Wait till you see."

They moved away at a pace she considered excessive, and she went slowly up to the house, wondering how the two incompatibles, grandmother and grandson, had met after the lapse of years. She wished she had been at home when Angus's letter had arrived; she would have liked to have seen Lady Evelyn's first reactions.

Lady Evelyn, observing her from a window, opened it and leaned out.

"Come along, my dear Anabelle; come along. So nice to have you back."

Anabelle went up the wide marble steps and walked into the hall. Then she paused, her eyes going slowly round the trophy-hung walls. She was seeing nothing that she had not seen countless times since her childhood—but for the first time she was attempting to view it through Angus Pemberton's eyes.

To enter the hall was to be transported with unnerving suddenness from a sleepy country town in

England to the barren, ever troubled area known as the North-West Frontier Province of India. Its mountains, its rivers and valleys were realistically reproduced on a vast contour map that occupied almost the whole of one wall. In a corner stood a life-size model of a Pathan, rifle pointed straight at the unprepared stranger entering the front door. Large paintings on another wall depicted gory battles between the turbaned and the topeed. Glass cases contained old and in some cases bloodstained uniforms, boots, saddles, and medals. In a central position facing the door hung a portrait of a bronzed, keen-eyed horseman in a picturesque green and gold uniform; a gilt-lettered notice below stated that he was Lord Quilling, founder and commander of the body of irregular cavalry known and honoured as Quilling's Horse—once, it was claimed, known and feared by every tribesman from Razmak to Chitral.

The exhibits had been arranged by Lady Evelyn. The only grandchild of the famous founder, she regarded herself not only heir to but also guardian of the brief but glorious history. Fired by a loyalty and enthusiasm that never grew cool, she had tried, without success, to transmit the spark to her son; after his death, she had turned to her grandson to find that he, like his father, was pure Pemberton and not to be won over to the Quilling legend. To Angus and his contemporaries, who thought of war in terms of tanks and Tommy guns, the long, unceasing, personally conducted tours of the hall had an embarrassingly musty flavour; that sort of thing, they felt, went out with Kipling.

Her efforts to force Angus into a military cast had driven a wedge between them and had at last resulted in his putting as much distance as possible between himself and his grandmother. And now, Anabelle mused, he was back. . . .

Lady Evelyn had come into the hall to greet her. Anabelle kissed the smooth, flaccid cheek and then stepped back to study the regal old lady.

"What have you done with that little boy you brought to England?" Lady Evelyn asked. "You and I are going to be busy and I'm not going to have him running loose in the house, especially in this hall."

"Don't worry." Anabelle smiled. "He won't."

"Angus told me that you brought him over because his grandfather was ill. Kind, no doubt—but wise? My dear, *no*. Far from wise. I remember my mother agreeing to have a French child for a fortnight, and what with one excuse and another it was months— *months*—before she could get rid of him. You really should have asked my advice before undertaking anything of the sort."

"Next time I will," Anabelle promised. "Now tell me about Angus."

"Well, you met him in Portugal and you traveled home with him, and so I don't have to tell you that he hasn't changed in one single particular."

"I thought he was glad to be coming home. He seemed—"

"Shall I tell you *why* he has come home? Not to see me; not to see his home again. He has come simply—I tell you this in strict confidence, mind—because he has been in communication with that snake Sanders."

She had seated herself angrily upon a wooden chair, carved, so the notice said, by a prisoner in Peshawar. Her cheeks were pink with annoyance.

"Old Mr. Sanders—a snake?" Anabelle asked in surprise.

"A serpent. I quarreled with him about a new will I wished him to draw up for me. He said it would ruin Angus's prospects and asked me to reconsider—and so I told him that I would get another lawyer. Naturally, since he has known Angus for nearly thirty years, he wrote off and told him what I had in mind —and Angus, who never in all his life cared a straw for me or for this house or for anything connected with it, has come back at top speed to make me change my mind and change my plans. As soon as he arrived I faced him with it; I knew quite well, I told him, what he had come for. He admitted it at once. He said nothing about Sanders, of course, but he said straight out that he had come to see that I didn't do anything I'd regret later. 'Later?' I said to him. 'Later? I shall be dead.' So he said that in *that* case he must see to it that I didn't do anything that *he* would regret later. I told him that he was too late; the papers were ready to sign—and *that*, he told me, was just the point at which the wicked grandson came home and made sure that Grandmother didn't live long enough to sign anything. He was . . . well, I suppose he was joking, but it was a joke in very bad taste. At all events I've put myself into Mr. Gravely's hands."

"Who's Mr. Gravely?"

"Of Gravely, Swift, and Gravely. They were my grandfather's solicitors in London and I should have asked them to act for me as soon as my husband died —but Sanders had always been the Pemberton lawyer, and I trusted him and so I remained with his firm. And now I'm sorry, because as soon as I told Mr. Gravely what I had in mind, he approved. Nothing that Angus can say or do will make me change my plans. Do you know what he told me this morning? That he was going to put the stables back into use. Do what you please, I said to him, but do it at your own expense. . . . But I won't talk about it any more, Anabelle; it's too bad to have him home again, upsetting me just as much as he did before." She rose. "Come along and let me show you all the things that people brought to the shop while you were away."

On entering the room, Anabelle felt grateful to Angus for having in some measure prepared her for the chaos that met her eyes. She stood on the threshold struggling against an impulse to turn and go home again, leaving Lady Evelyn to deal with the mess.

"Look at all those things they brought." Lady Evelyn was pointing them out. "Chairs, tables, rugs, two stoves, a washing machine, but I don't think it works; that lovely copper kettle, but it's got a hole, and those two dreadful pictures."

"You should have refused to take the kettle," Anabelle said. "And that stove too—who's going to buy that?"

"It's already sold," said Lady Evelyn.

The promptness of the reply, the slightly defiant

tone told Anabelle that the statement was untrue. Lady Evelyn had her own views on telling or not telling the truth; not telling it was sometimes the easiest way of avoiding tiresome argument. She could utter, without a blush, barefaced lies; challenged, she called them slips of the tongue.

"Who bought it?" Anabelle asked.

"I can't for the moment remember. Where have you left that little Portuguese boy? How long will he be staying?"

Anabelle ignored these obvious attempts to change the subject.

"I wish," she said, "I'd made you promise not to accept anything while I was away."

"That would have been silly. Come and look at this exquisite vase; it was brought in by that terrible old Mrs. Knowles. How, I asked her, *how* did she come to have such a beautiful thing in amongst her appalling trash—though of course I said it more tactfully."

"Then you're improving."

"My dear, at my age I cannot improve; I can only go on decaying. Who do you think brought in that old jug? None other than that detestable Mrs. Drage. She said she wanted twenty guineas for it because it was an heirloom. 'My dear, *dear* Mrs. Drage, I said to her, 'that jug is the one my husband and I gave you as a wedding present; I can point to the very place in which it had a crack.' Crack or not, it cost us every penny of ten guineas."

"Ten guineas?"

"Perhaps that was a slight slip of the tongue. We had enough expenses without being prodigal in the matter of wedding presents for people like the Drages."

"We'll price it at a guinea," Anabelle said.

Lady Evelyn was not listening.

"Anabelle, speaking of weddings, I had a rather good idea."

"Well?"

"It struck me that when Angus goes back to Brazil —because of course there will be nothing to keep him here—he ought to take a wife with him. A wife would steady him. He needs some nice English girl to run his home." She raised the gold-topped stick she always carried, and pointed it at Anabelle; then she brought it down to the floor with a triumphant thump. "Olivia!"

"When he was at home seven years ago," Anabelle reminded her, "you told me he wasn't very polite when you suggested—"

"Olivia has always said that she wanted to live in a warm climate; here is her chance. I shall talk to her; she has always been guided by me."

Anabelle let this serious misstatement pass. Nobody had ever succeeded in guiding Olivia. Nobody but Olivia guided Olivia.

While listening to Lady Evelyn, she had been tidying up; now she looked round with a frown.

"We need extra space," she pointed out. "Could you spare another room?"

"I had already thought of that. We could use it for china. Old Mr. Cope died and they brought all the china over here."

"To sell on commission?"

"No. A gift."

"Good. You didn't . . . you didn't send off any cheques to anybody?"

This was the chief cause of dissension between them. The sales took place, the money was placed in the bank, and at intervals Anabelle, after consultation with Lady Evelyn, sent a cheque to a chosen charity. But sometimes, carried away by success, Lady Evelyn answered appeals which Anabelle felt were less than deserving.

"I didn't send anything to anyone," Lady Evelyn declared. "Except a small sum to the five young men who are going to journey along the old Silk Route."

"The—"

"A splendid cause, if ever I heard of one. And—"

"But how—"

"—fraught with danger, as they pointed out to me in their letter. I don't know where the route is or where it goes to, but they assured me that even if they get *into* half the places on the way, it's doubtful if they'll ever get *out* again. Such enterprise, I thought, ought to be encouraged."

"Did you encourage anybody else?"

"No. Nobody. I did send a small, a negligible sum to those people who are trying to bring out some kind of head covering as a protection against nuclear fall-out or something of that kind; it seemed to me such a splendid idea."

"Is that a charity?"

"It's *encouragement*. Would you begrudge them these little sums?"

"Yes, I would." She glanced at her watch. "It's time to open shop."

The customers came. The kettle was sold by Lady Evelyn with instructions as to how to mend the hole; the china, two chairs, and mirror so large that they had despaired of ever getting rid of it, were disposed of. Anabelle, entering the last items in the books, tidied up, said goodbye, and went home.

Luis had not come in. She felt a sudden surge of hope; she had foreseen difficulties with regard to finding somewhere he could stay while she was at work, but if he and Angus continued to get on as well as they were doing now, the problem was as good as solved.

They came back at about seven. Anabelle was at the gate, waiting for them. The riders dismounted, and Luis, after thanking Angus excitedly, obeyed Anabelle's instructions to go into the house and change and have a shower.

"And test the temperature of the water *before* getting under it," she called after him.

"He can ride," Angus said. "Why were you waiting out here? Were we too late?"

"Not too late—but I expected you earlier."

"And felt worried?"

"A little."

"Why on earth—?"

"I don't know. Perhaps because Luis came mysteriously and might—"

"—vanish as mysteriously?"

"Something like that."

"And you'd miss him. In fact you're running yourself into bad trouble, because you'll soon be at the stage where his vanishing, mysteriously or openly, is going to tear a hole in your life."

"I'm fond of him. Who wouldn't be?"

"Who indeed; even my grandmother has begun to succumb to his small-boy charm."

"She saw him?"

"We came through the wood, and there she was."

"And—?"

"As I said, she rather took to him."

Her face lit up.

"What did she *say?*"

"Well, she asked him questions about his age and his attainments. The fact that he was a Catholic gave her pause, but when I explained to her that the present Pope was a well-meaning sort of chap, she said she was prepared to meet him halfway."

"What else?"

"Does it matter what she thinks of him?"

"Of course it matters! If she likes him, she'll allow him the run of the place when I can't find anywhere to leave him. You know quite well it matters. I might have known she'd like him; he's got—"

"—all the trimmings; quite." Angus spoke drily. "He snatched off his cap, slid off his pony, and kissed her hand. That showed, she said, that he'd been trained in essentials. Watching him, I could see just where I'd missed out. . . . Well, I must be off."

"I could give you a drink."

"You wouldn't be able to give me any attention until Luis was in bed. When do Keith and Clare get home?"

"In a few days, I think. Olivia's coming down on Friday. Are you coming in for that drink?"

"I'll have it with your father. It's a long time since I had a talk with him. Olivia, I hear, has grown into a beauty—but it's hard to believe." He opened the door for Anabelle and followed her into the house. "Anyway, I'll be glad to see her again."

And his grandmother would be glad if he was glad, she reflected, going upstairs to see Luis.

Chapter Five

ON FRIDAY AFTERNOON, on his way home after doing some errands in Steyne, Angus stopped his car at the traffic lights. Beside him coughed a scooter on which, glancing casually aside, he saw a pale, thin young man with a girl on the pillion seat. The next moment she had given a cry and, with an "Angus, darling!" had in two lithe movements deserted her companion and entered the car. The door slammed; the noise of horns in the rear told him that the light was green; he drove on.

"Well, well," he said. "Now I know what it feels like to be Perry Mason. Beautiful stranger . . ." He broke off and gave her a brief, sidelong scrutiny—and the next moment the car swerved so violently that the young man on the scooter, coming up behind them, let out a yell of protest.

"Hey! What's the idea?" he shouted, drawing level and glaring at Angus. "I nearly came in through your rear window."

Angus scarcely heard him.

"Olivia! I don't believe it."

"You didn't recognize me?"

She spoke absently, peering into a small mirror and adjusting her head scarf.

"*Recognize* you? Why—"

She was as fresh as the bright afternoon. She wore

clinging trousers, a shirt, and a short loose coat; she was completely at ease and totally oblivious of the escort she had abandoned.

"Your friend's calling you names," pointed out Angus.

"Oh—" She made a soft sound of impatience and leaned across him. "We're going to my house; just trail us, can't you?" she called.

"Trail you? Trail you? What's all this jumping on and jumping off and trailing you? And anyway, where do I go if I lose you?"

"Suit yourself," said Olivia. "Go on, Angus; don't take any notice of him. . . . It's nice to see you. Anabelle told me you were home."

He was, for once, at a loss. She had not been seated beside him for more than a few minutes, but they were enough to prove that she bore no resemblance whatever to the child he had known seven years ago. She was not merely a woman; she was Woman, with a capital.

"Can't you talk?" she asked him.

"Presently. I'm thinking."

"If it's about me, keep at it."

"It's about you. What made you turn out so different from your sisters?"

"My sisters? I didn't want to know nothing, like Clare, and I didn't want to stay home and do nothing, like Anabelle. So I got out and grew up."

"I see. Are you like this all through, or is it only a . . . a patina?"

"Patina means rust; try again. It isn't a façade, if that's what you want to say. It goes right through. I'm not dressed up to look adult; I am."

He believed it. He wondered how it was that some women, merely by sitting and doing nothing, could create tension in the air around them. Who would have believed that this sophisticate had grown up in that homely little garden next door?

"Fellow on the scooter still behind us?" he asked.

Olivia glanced over her shoulder.

"Yes."

"Who is he?"

"Nobody special. He's in my group at the art school."

"What's his name?"

"We call him Artie."

"Is he going to stay with you?"

"No, at the pub."

When Angus drew up at the Bairds' front door, Artie, without getting off his scooter, shuffled awkwardly forward until he was abreast of them.

"I should have strapped her down, like the luggage," he told Angus without rancour.

In his swollen driving suit and grotesque helmet, his nose purple and moist, he looked anything but prepossessing—but the smile Olivia gave him was not derisive but indulgent. It proved to Angus that at least something of the old Olivia remained—a trace of the maternal feelings so strong in her sister Anabelle.

Anabelle, making tea for them all, listened to Angus's description of the meeting and took it as an indication that fate was playing on Lady Evelyn's side. Tea over, the scooter roared away, Olivia once more on the pillion. Angus stared after it thoughtfully.

"Well, no wonder you left me to see for myself," he said.

She made no reply. To Clare and to herself, the success achieved by the end product was less remarkable than the care and labour with which it had been built. Olivia had done it under their wondering and admiring eyes; they were less impressed by what she had become than how she had become. Her fringe came off with the wide ribbon that held it in place; her pony tail was detachable, as were the smooth topknot she wore in the evening and the curving lashes that arched above her serene dark eyes. Her figure was slim or padded, according to the type of dress she was wearing. The overall effect was, astonishingly, one of complete simplicity; hers was indeed the art that concealed art.

"What's underneath it all?" Angus enquired. "She claims that it goes right through. Right through or not, she's the type that used to be labeled Safer Married. This Artie looks an unlikely sort of escort for her."

"She admires his work."

"What surprises me is that my grandmother hasn't got busy fixing her up with someone. . . . Where's Luis?"

"Guess."

"Stables?"

"No. School."

"*School!*"

She was glad to see him, for once, shaken out of his calm.

"Yes. Mrs. Swann's."

He was staring at her.

"But . . . but good Lord, how long do you imagine he's going to be here?"

"I don't know—but he can't hang round doing nothing. I asked my father if he thought it would be a good idea to try and get him into Mrs. Swann's. I saw her yesterday and she had a look at Luis, and so there he is—at school."

"Liking it?"

"Well, he *went*. I took him there, but in future he can take himself." She gave a smile of satisfaction. "It shows he's lost his feeling of strangeness."

"He didn't appear to me to have any."

"But he did—at first. On the ship . . ."

She stopped. It was only too easy to talk like this. It was only too easy to forget how he had come, why he had come, how long it would be before he was taken away. He was already a member of the family; she knew, her father knew his moods, his virtues, and his failings; they had become used to the contrast between his unusual self-control in some situations and his tendency to howl at the slightest bodily ailment. He had the ability to sense exactly the right touch in his dealings with grownups; he was silent with Mr. Baird, he chattered with Lady Evelyn, he was on easy and friendly terms with the daily woman and with the tradesmen who came to the house. With other children he was usually bored; how he would react to their constant proximity at school she had yet to see.

"How long's Olivia staying?" Angus asked.

They were back to Olivia. . . .

"Two weeks, I think."

"And Artie?"

"He's going back on Sunday evening or on Monday morning."

"Well, I can't offer Olivia a scooter, but perhaps she'll consider my car. It ought to prove an instructive couple of weeks; I've been too long away from her type. If she gets too irresistible, how would you care for me as a brother-in-law?"

The question brought her to the surprised realization that if it had been put a short while ago, she would have answered with a decided and not polite negative. Today she knew that at some time since that day on which they had boarded the *Yeoman,* her feeling for him had undergone a basic and rather disconcerting change. She liked him; in the matter of Luis, she leaned on him. How much she liked, how much she leaned was something that she had not cared to ask herself.

She looked up to see surprise in his eyes.

"Why the hesitation?"

"Keith set a rather high standard in brothers-in-law."

"I see. I thought for a moment . . . Well, never mind. Why didn't you wait until Monday before sending Luis to school?"

"Mrs. Swann wanted a try-out; she said if Friday didn't go well, there wouldn't be any Monday."

"I hope he makes it. But he will; look what he's done to my grandmother."

They both laughed—so long and so helplessly that Mr. Baird, working in his room upstairs, hoped that he would remember to ask what the joke had been.

"But why," Anabelle asked, sobering, "why couldn't you have been like Luis? All small boys adore being soldiers; couldn't you have—"

"It's different for Luis. He wasn't reared in the tradition. He didn't have to listen, all his life, to tales of the not-Vienna but-Khyber Woods. He didn't have to salute the illustrious founder's portrait in the hall every morning. He didn't find himself dressed, at every wedding at which he was a page, or at every fancy dress party, in a green and gold uniform, complete with tin sword. He didn't have to go to church on the tenth of December to commemorate the whatever-it-was anniversary of Quilling's Cavalry. He didn't have a dead weight of dead history hung onto his shoulders and he didn't—"

"All right. I've got the idea."

He pulled himself together.

"You see? Even talking about it makes me see red."

"Green and gold."

"Green and gold. Have you discovered, or has my grandmother told you what brought me home?"

"Yes. The fact that she was changing her will."

"Old Sanders wrote to me. He shouldn't have written to me—but as she threw him out, he thought he ought to warn me that she'd gone to the old Quilling lawyers and instructed them to draw up papers for what she's going to call the Quilling Trust. I asked her point-blank, and—after a few slips of the tongue—she told me the truth. The house is to be a memorial for Quilling's Cavalry, disbanded God only knows how many years ago, and never more than a collection of heroes—heroes they were, I'm not denying it—who rallied round a rich man who was indulging his passion for soldiering on his own pattern. The house is to be a memorial, and the money—my money—will go to keep the memory green—and gold."

"Her money."

"*My* money. My father's, my grandfather's, his father's and grandfather's; mine, my son or sons', my grandson or grandsons'. It was never Quilling money. All the Quilling money went on Quilling's Cavalry. After that it was Pemberton money. When my grandmother married my grandfather, all she had was her title and the Quilling legend. Now she proposes to devote my patrimony—I use the word in its real sense—to founding a museum, or a memorial, or both. Which would be all right with me—I think, though I'm not sure—if the descendants of the heroes showed any interest in remembering. But they didn't and they don't. Years ago, when I was about eighteen or so, I wondered if perhaps my grandmother saw something in the legend that I'd missed—and so I went through all the old papers and I made a list of all the descendants I could trace and wrote to every single one of them. The response was so faint that you couldn't have heard it with a hearing-aid. Quilling was a brave man and I'm proud of him, but I don't propose to let my grandmother donate my patrimony and hand over my house to fan a spark that went out long ago. She knows what my views are; I told her."

"You can't stop her from signing."

"You mean, I suppose, that I can't resort to violence or to blackmail."

"I mean that what you're up against isn't an impulse she's just had. She must have been thinking of something like this for years—in fact, ever since she faced the fact that you took after your father and not after your grandfather. And you can't use violence—and what is there to blackmail her *about?*"

"When you come to think of it, old age is a kind of blackmail in itself. And not allowing the heir to inherit until he's thirty is another form of blackmail. It was my grandmother who instituted the system; suppose Grandfather Pemberton gave in for the sake of peace, but it's quite certain he'd never have agreed to it if he'd known that my father would die before he reached thirty and leave my grandmother in sole charge of the assets. If people turn in their graves, the old man's turning now. If my grandmother hadn't decided to commemorate Quilling's Cavalry, she would have hit on some other way of disposing of my inheritance, because she has to have a Cause, capital C. But why do I tell you? You know her almost as well as I do."

"What would happen if you went up to London and talked to Mr. Gravely?"

"He wouldn't see me. And Sanders can do nothing. So my grandmother will do what she wants to do— unless I stop her. I'll certainly have a damn good try."

And might, she thought, succeed. The seven years

had given him authority; perhaps he had learned how to handle the imperious old lady.

"She's—" she began and stopped. The telephone in the hall had shrilled, and she went to answer it. Outside the house, he could hear her voice.

"*Philip!* But where? . . . *When?* Yes, of course; yes, I will. . . . Roughly what time? Yes . . . Yes, of course. Goodbye."

Angus, leaning against the door that led to the kitchen, spoke casually as she put down the receiver.

"Call from Lisbon?"

"Lisbon? No, he's here. I mean he's at London Airport. He's coming down by car; he wants me to ring his house and tell the housekeeper he's on his way."

"How long's he staying?"

"Two days. He's just over to . . ."

She did not complete the sentence. She had written to tell him that what her views had been, her views still were, but she would do nothing to make trouble between him and the Jansens; if he, or they, or he and they decided to put off the wedding, she would agree. And as she wrote, she had been aware that she no longer had any strong feelings about what he did, or what the Jansens did. . . .

He was here, and the fact that he had come in this headlong, completely uncharacteristic way might mean that the indifference she had felt, and which she had tried to keep out of the letter, had nevertheless communicated itself to him.

Lost in speculation, she refused absently Angus's offer to fetch Luis from school. Watching him go away, she had a sudden, crazy impulse to call him back and appeal to him for help as she had done on the *Yeoman.* But in this matter, she remembered, he would be the last person to whom she could go for help.

When she was alone, she rang up the woman who worked for Philip's mother, acting as willing caretaker when Philip and his mother were away, and as willing cook-housekeeper when they were at home.

"Tonight?" came the surly voice over the wire. "Not much notice, is it? What does 'e think I keep in the house—sides of beef and a supply of deep-freeze? 'E'll have ter eat out if 'e turns up tonight."

"He'll dine here. Would you please get his room ready?"

"I'll make 'is bed, if that's what you mean."

"Thank you. You might also see that there's hot water, which you forgot to do last time. I'll send eggs and bacon for his breakfast. And if you're using the drawing room to watch television, please see that your undergarments aren't hanging in front of the fire to dry, as they were last time Mr. Ancell came home. That's all."

And please remember, she continued aloud, putting down the receiver with a crash, please note that if ever I have to live in that house, the first thing I'll throw out will be you, cotton combinations and all.

Olivia came back on Artie's scooter. She went up to her room and came down a short while later wearing a jacket and trousers that looked to Anabelle like a matador's outfit without the trimmings.

"What did you do with the bull?" she enquired.

"Left him at the pub, settling in." Olivia went to the refrigerator, helped herself to a cool drink, found and opened a tin of nuts, and settled herself comfortably on a stool.

"How about peeling the vegetables for dinner?" Anabelle suggested.

"You do it and I'll watch. I wanted to ask you about this little Portuguese boy you seem to be landed with. How long's he staying?"

"I don't know."

"Where's he now?"

"At school."

"School! That makes him sound pretty permanent."

"I thought he ought to have something to do, so I took him round to Mrs. Swann."

"You mean she still runs that kindergarten? She must be all of ninety. Remember how she used to put the fear of God into us all?"

"I remember."

"Then why throw Luis into her lap?"

"He'll survive. . . . Do you want me to give Artie meals, or will he eat at the pub?"

"Pub. We can have a nice, quiet family dinner."

"We can't. Philip's here."

"*Here?*"

The tone was one of undisguised horror. Whatever her reasons for having become engaged to Philip had been, Anabelle reflected, pleasing her family had not been one of them.

"He's at London Airport. More accurately, he's on his way down here."

"Can you beat it?" Olivia asked bitterly. "I come down after months, and I choose the week-end he chooses. But what's he here *for?* You've only just left him in Portugal."

"We had a row. Perhaps he's come to make it up."

Olivia blew the salt off a handful of nuts and scooped them into her mouth.

"Take my advice and widen the breach into a chasm he can't get across," she said. "I couldn't stand him in the same room, let alone the same bed. Sure you know what you're doing?"

"Not as sure as I was."

"Then open the door when he arrives, hand him the ring, and shut and bolt the door again. Marrying's enough to daunt anyone—all that ghastly housekeeping and cooking men-meals—why can't men live off salads and things, as we do?—and babies, if you get careless; the only reason for going through with it is because you've found a man you think is worth it—but who'd want to take it on with anybody like Philip? Think it over; this may be your chance to call it off. When's he arriving?"

"Some time around eight-thirty, I suppose."

"Then I'll get Angus to take me out somewhere."

"Angus? What about Artie?"

"Are you serious? Do you think I'd waste time with Artie when Angus is around?"

"You brought him down here."

"Correction: he brought me down here. He said he wanted a week-end in the country, which he imagined Steyne was. I gave him the address of the pub, he

got a room there, and now what? I have to give up my
week-end trying to make a success of his?" She
pushed the tin across the table. "Here, have a nut. I'm
going over to the big house to look for Angus."

"On Artie's scooter? In that getup?"

"First you worry about Artie; now you're wor-
rying about Lady Evelyn. Honestly, Anabelle, people
can look after themselves."

The scooter came to life, sent shafts of agony
through Mr. Baird's head, and faded into the distance.
Ten minutes later, Artie appeared at the kitchen door.

"Thought I'd come round this way," he explained.
"Any sign of Olivia and my scooter?"

"They came—and went."

"Went where?"

"To see Lady Evelyn." Truth was truth, but kindness was still kindness. "I don't think she'll be long."

"Oh. Mind if I hang round?"

"Not at all."

She handed him a newspaper, but he put it aside.
He watched her idly as she rolled pastry and draped
it over a pie; he hung over her to watch her put it into
the oven. Whistling softly, he wandered out of the
kitchen and she heard him punishing the piano. Closing the lid with a crash, he tried in turn Olivia's guitar, Clare's long discarded recorder, and a zither that,
lacking players, had been retained as ornament. Wandering into the hall, he tried on the miscellaneous collection of hats hanging on pegs in the cloakroom; returning to the kitchen, he opened and closed cup-
boards in aimless fashion, picked up and absently ate a
hard-boiled egg Anabelle had just shelled, and finished
the tin of nuts that Olivia had opened.

"If I were you," Anabelle suggested in desperation,
"I'd walk over and meet Olivia."

" 'M I in your way?"

"No, but—"

"Mind if I try a slice of that ham?"

"No. Do take some."

He cut two slices of bread, buttered them liberally,
and put the ham between them. Eating, he performed
a slow and complicated dance round the kitchen,

treading on the scarlet tiles and carefully avoiding the
pale blue and the white.

"Shouldn't eat between meals, but you put temptation in my way," he observed. "Funny that Olivia
hasn't done you a mural on one of these walls. That's
how I first got keen on art—doing murals at home. I
knew I was good, but I couldn't get anybody to believe it, because nobody knew what the pictures were
supposed to represent. Then one of my crazy aunts
dropped in, looked at the walls, screeched loudly, and
galloped off to fetch an art critic, and the next thing I
knew, I was in a room in London—art student. So
. . . You going out?"

"I was going to fetch a little boy from school."

Artie strapped on his helmet.

"I'll go. Just tell me where."

She told him and, with deep relief, saw him depart.
If Olivia was going to abandon him, he would have to
kick his heels somewhere else and not in this kitchen.

He came back with Luis and also brought a message to the effect that Olivia would be dining out—
with him. This supplied the information that Angus
had not been at home, having driven over to Outersteyne to look at horses.

Philip arrived at nine; Luis was in bed, Mr. Baird
had dined and retired to his room. She and Philip had
a late dinner together and then they moved into the
drawing room for coffee.

She thought him quiet, almost subdued on his arrival, but drinks before dinner seemed to revive him,
and by the end of dinner he was almost talkative—but
he had not touched upon Portugal, or the Jansens, or
wedding dates. It was Anabelle who decided at last to
approach the subject.

"Did you talk to the Jansens?" she asked.

"Of course I did." He smiled, rose from the sofa,
and brought his coffee cup to her to be refilled. "Isn't
that why I'm here now?"

"What did they say?"

He drank the coffee before replying; then he put
down the cup and waved an indulgent hand.

"They were wonderful; no reproaches, nothing but

a complete willingness to look at it from your point of view. They ironed the whole thing out in no time."

She had schooled herself to patience and control—but his tone, smug, insufferable, brought her to her feet and sent her to the long window and out into the cool garden.

There was a moon—almost a full moon. From time to time, clouds drifted across it, so that the house was at one moment bathed in soft light and the next moment velvety black save for the broad shaft of light from the drawing room and the glow from her father's window above.

Philip followed her out and stood beside her.

"You mustn't think about that silly quarrel," he said. "We've all decided to forget all about it."

"Who's 'we'?"

"Karl and Karen and I."

"Karl and Karen?"

"They felt that calling them by the surname was silly. I'd been thinking so for some time, as a matter of fact, but I hadn't liked to be the first to say so. If the suggestion came at all, it had to come from them. Don't you agree?"

It was better to agree silently. It was better not to speak.

He noticed nothing ominous in the silence. The drinks before dinner, the warm soup, the succulent chicken pie, the excellent wine Mr. Baird had extracted from the cavity under the hall floor boards that was known as the cellar; fresh fruit, good coffee, a night cool after rain; all these had combined to give him a confidence he had not felt on arrival.

"Karl and Karen and I went into, as you might say, committee," he explained. "They . . . You're not chilly out here?"

"No. Go on."

"Well, we talked, the three of us, when I got back from the Prendergasts'. They were awfully kind, both of them. I was pretty tired, you know, after that week-end; I hadn't liked to say anything to you, because they were your friends, but I found it all, frankly, rather more than I could take. All that shouting, not a quiet second to oneself, and to crown it all, Pemberton hanging round. Is he here, by the way?"

"Yes. Go on."

"As I say, we had it out when I got back to Lisbon. I put it quite frankly to Karl and to Karen: she *has*, you understand, I told them, a say in this matter. They quite agreed. So what we worked out was this: that we'd approach the matter by a system of priorities. Priority number one, naturally, our wedding. That must come first. The thing, as Karen pointed out—she's intelligent, Anabelle, as you'll find out when you get to know her better—the thing was not to put the wedding *off* but to put it *on*. And so here I am. We marry as soon as we can fix our details. I know it means no splash and just ourselves and our immediate families, but you've always said that you didn't want a big wedding. Special license, church if you like. I've got two weeks as from today. We marry; we have, shall we say, half a honeymoon; we go to Rome, I open the office, and perhaps after Christmas I could ask Karl for another week and we could stay on in Rome—I might even look into the office mornings only, or something of that kind—or we could take a short trip somewhere. . . . Well— what d'you say to that?"

There was silence. He did not hurry her.

"I couldn't marry you straightaway, Philip," she said quietly at last.

"Well"—he laughed—"I didn't mean we'd walk out first thing in the morning and get married. But you could do it within the week, couldn't you?"

"No, I couldn't."

The moon was behind a cloud, but she could hear the frown in his voice.

"But—but why not? You're not going to raise objections this time too, are you?"

"How could I leave Luis?"

"Luis? *Luis?* Who the devil . . . ? Oh, that Portuguese child! Good heavens, do you really seriously mean—"

"I told you in my letter that he was staying here."

"Well, send him home again."

"I can't send him home."

"Why the devil not?"

"His . . . his grandfather's ill. He's to stay here until he gets better."

The moon, reappearing, illuminated his face, puckered with anger.

"I don't get this," he said. "Frankly you've got me in a fog. When I left you in Portugal, you didn't, as far as I could see, know a soul except the Prendergasts. Now you tell me you're stuck with a Portuguese child because his grandfather is ill. Who's his grandfather? How did you meet him? Where did you meet him? What's he to you? How could this arrangement, which must have been hashed up in the last few days of your stay, interfere with your plans, your marriage, your life, our life? Where's the problem? You send a wire, or you phone and say, you've got to send him back. I'll drive him to the airport, if you like, and put him aboard, and they can arrange to have him taken off at the other end."

"I can't send him back."

"You can but"—his tone was tense—"you won't. All right. if you don't want to cut his holiday short, ask Clare to take him. You've thrown in my face for years the fact that if you looked after her children now, she'd do the same for us later. Well, here's her chance: tell her to look after this Luis or whatever his name is."

"Clare's not here."

"Do I have to tell Karl and Karen—because I promised I'd ring up and let them know our wedding date as soon as I'd talked to you—do I have to tell them that we can't get married because you've got a Portuguese brat on your hands? Anabelle, talk sense!"

"I'm sorry. I know it sounds . . . less than sensible, but there it is."

"How long do you think I'll put up with this I-won't and I-can't? What sort of position does this put me into? I try to put off the wedding; no, you won't. I offer to put forward the wedding; no, you can't. Last time we disagreed, it was you who issued an ultimatum. This time I won't call it an ultimatum, but I will say that I'm not going to agree to sabotaging all Karen's plans just because you have crazy ideas of housing foreign children. I shall go home, and you can think it over."

"I don't have to think it over. I can't marry you now."

"And you can't marry me at the end of the year. When *do* we get married?—if we do get married and all this isn't a big stall while you're lining up somebody else."

"I'd take that back, if I were you."

"All right; I take it back—but put to the Jansens, it'll look just that. Try and make them believe that I'm being held up by a Portuguese child you couldn't have set eyes on two or three weeks ago."

"I don't think I'll waste time trying."

"That's a nice tone to take! I've gone to the trouble of having it out with the Jansens; I've agreed with them that this is the best thing to be done. I've come all this way to fall in with what I was certain would be what you wanted. . . ."

"Whether I wanted it or not doesn't matter. I can't marry you this week or next. And something else: Luis or no Luis, I resent being hurried to the altar just as much as I resented the suggestion to put off the wedding."

"In other words, anything the Jansens want is all wrong with you?"

"That's it."

"It sticks out three miles—which, come to think of it, is the limit, and that's what we've reached, I think." His voice had risen to an angry falsetto. "I'm sorry I didn't consult you before choosing my Chief. I'm sorry you don't like his wife—but if you're interested, she's been a better mother to me than my own mother ever was. And if you don't like Karl and Karen, I don't like having my wedding held up by a boy I never heard you mention in my life before. If that's the only reason you can produce for not marrying me, you'd better think again. *Is* there another reason?"

"Well, only one." She took a deep breath, went

down in an exploratory dive, and came up with the truth she had been keeping submerged for so long. "I don't love you."

"Ah! So we've got there at last! Karen said you'd come out with it in the end."

"Did she? Then you were right; she's intelligent."

"So our little Luis was nothing but a stall after all? He was a red herring, a—"

"Catalyst is the word you want."

"I suppose you understand what you're doing? I won't come back, you know."

"I hope you won't. Karen will explain that it's better to make a—I think she'll call it a clean break."

"I wish I'd had the sense to see through you earlier. She told me this would happen. Coming out with those boys, she said, in spite of being warned to leave them behind—that showed that you weren't really concerned with what was best for me."

"Did you really let her talk like that about me?"

"I told you; she looked on me as a son. She said—"

"She's probably waiting to say a whole lot more. Go back to Mother. Do you want your ring now, or shall I post it?"

"I don't want the ruddy ring."

"I'll post it. Goodbye. I'm sorry you had your journey for nothing—but Karl will refund the fare."

"I feel it only fair to tell you that if I go now it'll be the end."

"So you said. Goodbye. Please go away."

He went away. She heard him slam the door of the house and the door of the car. He turned right and not left at the end of the drive, which meant that he was not going to his mother's house; he was going back to the airport to await the first available plane back to Karl and Karen. The housekeeper had moved her underwear for nothing.

She felt relief, and something else: a wave of loneliness. She was adrift—she and Luis. Something must happen soon; things could not be left as they were. . . .

But for the moment, relief could predominate. Philip had gone.

She turned to go into the house and then halted abruptly. From the other side of the wall came the sound of a cough. It was discreet, it was apologetic. It was also admonitory. And familiar.

Without warning, she burst suddenly into tears. The next moment, Angus Pemberton's penitent countenance appeared over the dividing wall; with no hesitation, he levered himself up, seized and pulled the branch of a tree, and swung himself clear of the holly hedge. Without words, he took her in a close, brotherly embrace and held her while sobs shook her body and choked her.

When at last she was quiet, he substituted his clean handkerchief for her sodden one and spoke in a matter-of-fact tone.

"You're sorry you sent him away? Shall I fetch him back?"

"No. I don't want him back."

"Pity you promised to return that ring; he must have paid a packet for it. No girl I ever knew behaved so scrupulously."

She drew herself out of his arms.

"I'm sorry I howled."

"Did you good. Odd that this should be the first time I've ever jumped the fence and taken any of you into my arms. A habit which, once established, mustn't be allowed to lapse. But returning for a moment to your recent fiancé, isn't he entitled to complain when you push him to one side on account of a small boy for whom you've no real responsibility?"

"You were listening, weren't you? Didn't you hear me tell him—"

"—that you weren't in love with him? Yes, I heard. It was most convincingly said. He'll need all the comfort Karen can give him. But it makes my position very difficult."

"I wouldn't have said you had a position."

"Use your imagination. Man returns to ancestral home, struck by amazing change in neighbouring maidens. Only one maiden free, so no problem. Two now free, therefore serious problem."

"You keep after Olivia," she advised him coldly. "You'll make a good pair."

"You wouldn't consider me?"

"No."

"Reconsider," he begged. "My supposed instability, and your splendid sound sense—which is, since we're speaking frankly, even more legendary than my lack of virtue. Since I've met you, you've shown yourself willing to get involved not only in an engagement that should never had been entered into, but also in a situation full of who can tell how many sinister possibilities. You've fortunately freed yourself from the man, but you're still stuck with the boy—and whichever way that situation ends, you lose, because you've let yourself become hopelessly caught up emotionally."

"Finished?" she enquired.

"By no means. I'm outlining my problem: Olivia the sexy, the disturbing but essentially self-sufficient; or you, so prone to fall into other people's troubles?"

"I've solved your problem for you: keep after Olivia."

His reply was to take her once more into his arms. This time there was nothing brotherly about the embrace—or about the lips that rested for so long upon her own.

She made no resistance. His body was broader, stronger, far more accommodating than Philip's. Leaning against him, she could sense the strength and the power that Philip had never possessed. She had a feeling of warmth—a warmth that pervaded her, that began to course through her and quicken her heartbeats.

Abruptly, at last, she broke away.

She heard him speaking calmly.

"Too late," he said. "Too late, that is, to pretend any more. You know—and I know. I knew as soon as I saw you on Lisbon Airport. You didn't know until you were in my arms just now. Funny, isn't it, to think that for seven years I hardly remembered you?"

"I remembered you."

"But not kindly." He took her face between his

hands and studied it by the light from the house. "Let me see how a girl like you looks when a man tells her that he loves her."

"You're . . . you're going too fast," she said.

"Am I?" His arms slipped around her. "Am I? Perhaps"—he released her slowly—"perhaps I am. Perhaps I ought to give you a night to get used to the idea. Or will you spend it remembering the years in which you regarded me as—"

"Angus . . ."

"Well?"

"I don't know. Just that I'm . . . frightened."

"You weren't frightened when I kissed you just now."

"No. But—but isn't that what you always do to women when you kiss them? You didn't seem to me —you weren't exactly out of practice."

"If you're interested—and I feel that you are— you're the only woman who has ever meant anything to me. Except one."

"And . . . and she?"

"She's dead. It was a long time ago, and since then —nobody. Nobody until I flew into Lisbon and saw you . . . saw you down there with the two children and realized that I'd come home." He bent and kissed her lightly. "Declaration coming. I love you. I love you very much."

She felt tears pouring down her cheeks and did nothing to check them.

"Did you hear? I love you."

"Th-thank you," she sobbed.

"Don't thank me; just think it over. Why are you crying again?"

"I . . . I don't know."

He dried her tears and kissed her. He opened the door and put her gently inside the house and spoke softly.

"Sleep well, my love."

Chapter Six

SHE SLEPT LITTLE that night. The hours went slowly by, and she was aware that they should have been happy hours—but she was lost in misery and bewilderment. She loved him, and he had told her that he loved her; while he had been with her, she had found it easy to believe him—but he had gone, and she was left with the fear of having read too much into the brief incident, of having magnified it, of having misinterpreted it and given it much more importance than he had meant it to have.

She had been in his arms—but so had other women. His power to charm was a byword. Crowding into her mind came all that she had heard of him, all that people said of him.

A light touch . . . To meet, to kiss, to part. Clare and Olivia had always had the technique; she had always lacked it. She knew that for them, there had been many moonlit sessions, even many passionate declarations—all taken, in Clare's words, for what they were worth, which was usually very little.

Her fear of having mistaken Angus's words and actions grew stronger with the dawn. She longed to see him—longed to meet him and to gauge how much last night had meant to him. The day would show whether the night had been only a dream.

She went downstairs early. The post had arrived;

she saw addressed to herself a long, thick envelope. Opening it, she drew out five new, unfolded notes of ten pounds each. There was no letter. The postmark was Oporto.

She took them up to her father with his morning tea. He pushed aside the morning papers and counted the notes thoughtfully.

"Fifty," she said. "It would be interesting to know how long the money's meant to last. In fact, it would be interesting to know anything."

"Are you regretting—"

"No. What is there to regret? He's well and he's happy and he's a member of the family. Angus likes him and Lady Evelyn loves him. Mrs. Swann has agreed to take him."

"But someday, someone will take him away."

"I know but what's the use of anticipating? What do you think I ought to do with the money?"

Mr. Baird pondered.

"It would buy a pony for Luis. That one he's riding—Mawson would probably let you have it for less than fifty pounds, and he'd stable it, as he did the pony that you girls had."

"Angus would stable it. But you're paying for Luis's keep; I ought to give you the money."

"No. Buy the pony."

"Very well." She hesitated. "There's something else."

He peered up at her.

"My dear, is it about your engagement?"

"Yes. I saw your light was on; I suppose you heard us?"

"I could have shut my window, but I thought you would hear me and feel embarrassed."

"Lady Evelyn will be glad. So will Keith and Clare. So will Olivia—and you, I suppose."

Mr. Baird poured out a cup of tea and embarked upon a mild defense.

"To be taken up by those people—the Jansens—must have been a new and pleasant experience for Philip," he said. "Nobody paid much attention to him when he was young. I'm glad you're not going to marry him, but I don't think I ever felt it would come to marriage; he is an irritating man and your temper is not always under control, and lately I knew you were beginning to realize that you'd made a mistake. But hearing you quarreling last night, I sat up here wondering if perhaps I shouldn't have sent you away long ago—by which I mean, of course, that I should have urged you to go away from Steyne, which is a very small and very dull town. Perhaps you would think over the question now. If Clare is going to have a home in London, perhaps you could—"

She was no longer listening; her mind was busy with the chilling realization that her father had heard not only the quarrel with Philip but also its sequel—and far from making any reference to it, he was urging her to leave Steyne and, presumably, look for a husband elsewhere. It was, she felt certain, an oblique comment, his way of showing her how little importance he attached to it. He had overheard the exchange, and he had judged it to have no significance—and with that realization came another even more humiliating—the memory of how little Angus had uttered in the future tense.

About her own feelings she had no illusions. The few moments last night in the garden had had, for her, a depth and meaning that had changed her life. She was in love—deeply and irrevocably. Last night she had had no doubt that Angus loved her; now, faced with her father's total disregard of what had taken place, she forced herself to face the bitter facts.

He could beguile women—and what was she but a woman; yet another woman?

She left her father and went quietly downstairs. Luis, she saw, had eaten the breakfast she had left for him; he had gone out and she could guess where. Olivia was not yet down, and she decided to go up and ask whether she would like her coffee in bed—but as she turned to the door, it opened and Olivia entered. She was dressed in a jacket and jodhpurs; her wild hair and pink cheeks were indications that she had already been out.

"I thought you weren't up," Anabelle said in surprise.

"Up? I was up and out by seven. I've been over at Mawson's with Angus, trying out horses."

Anabelle stared at her.

"When did he . . . when did you . . . ?"

"He threw gravel up at my window and woke me. I've often read about people doing that, but I didn't know how it worked. Now I know."

There was a pause.

"Breakfast now or when you've changed?" Anabelle asked quietly.

She was not surprised at the calmness of her tone. She felt entirely calm. The short, sharp tempest of emotion was over; she needed nothing now but time to adjust herself to the idea that she was not, after all, any different from any other woman; lower the lights, play soft music, bring on the hero with the well-thumbed script, and that was all that was needed to convince the lonely girl that she was the only girl.

It was a lesson—a hard lesson, but she was prepared to learn. Her father—and Olivia; two successive showers of cold water to shock her out of her dreams and to brace her to confront Angus Pemberton with a coolness that would match his own.

"I'll change first," Olivia said.

She came down in a light woolen dress, poured out her coffee and opened a newspaper.

"Any special news?" she asked.

"Only domestic. I'm not engaged any more."

Olivia put down the paper and looked at her round-eyed.

"You really mean it's off?"

"Yes."

"Congratulations. Did you tell Father?"

"I didn't have to; his window was open and he heard it all."

"But he came all the way from Portugal—"

"He came home with a proposition to get married at once. I said I couldn't. Luis was an excuse, and a good one, but not the real one."

"If you want my opinion, here it is: you're well out of it."

"Angus knew. Didn't he say anything to you this morning?"

"Not a word. All he talked about was horses. Where is Luis, by the way?"

"Over with Lady Evelyn, I think."

"I'm going across after breakfast."

"What about Artie?"

"If he turns up, he can come too."

Artie arrived five minutes later; he had been, he told them, for a long walk and would be grateful for any breakfast that happened to be going spare.

"Coffee and toast?" Anabelle asked.

"Thanks." He sat down, his face the picture of satisfaction. "People ought to get out of town more. I feel a different chap since Friday. I like that pub, too; nice room and decent food and a lot of going and coming to keep you from feeling dull. Funny thing: a chap came up to me asking if I wanted to buy a dog. I wish you could have seen it! Man, I told him, if I wanted a dog, which in a back room in a back street in London I don't, I wouldn't buy a dog like that one; I'd buy one I could fit. The one he was trying to sell was a cross between a Shetland pony and a Highland heifer. It was shaggy, and it stood all of four feet high."

"How much did he want for it?" Olivia asked.

"Three quid. If he'd let the thing off its chain, it would have cleared everybody off the street in three minutes flat. Could I make myself another piece of toast?"

"No. We're going out," Olivia said.

"Where to?"

"Over to Steyne House."

"I'll go with you," Anabelle said.

She did not want to go. She did not have to go, for she was free on Saturdays—but there were some cheques to be written; if she did not write them, Lady Evelyn would—but not to the chosen charities. She shrank from seeing Angus, but she would have to meet him sooner or later; let it be sooner.

They walked through the woods towards the big house, and long before they saw her they were made aware of Lady Evelyn's presence by the series of sharp, shrill commands issuing from the terrace.

"Left, right; left, right; left, right. Halt! No, no, no, Luis; I *told* you, dear boy; halt means *stop*. Now try again. Ready?"

She was standing on the top step of a shallow stone flight. Luis was drilling on the terrace below. Her voice was not made for shouting, but for the sergeant's bark she had substituted a staccato yap that carried almost as far. She was as little pleased by the interruption as Luis.

"What's the idea?" the mystified Artie asked as they approached. "Wolf cubs or something?"

"Quilling's Cavalry, Unmounted," Olivia said.

"What's that?"

"You'll learn."

"Left, right; left, right. Halt! Dis-miss."

"Why? I'm not tired," protested Luis. "I can do more."

"Well, all these people have come to see me. And didn't Angus say he was going to take you over to Mr. Mawson's stables?"

"Then after can I do more?"

She flushed with pleasure.

"Certainly, certainly; we shall do much more, Luis. Good morning, Anabelle; I suppose you want me to sign cheques?"

"Yes, please. I'm just going to write them. Lady Evelyn, this is Mr. Bond."

"How do you do, Mr. . . . Good morning, Olivia. Oh, by the way, Anabelle, I have good news for you; I sold the Windsor chair for eight pounds."

"Not selling up, are you?" Artie asked in surprise.

"Are you interested in buying anything, Mr.—?"

"Artie Bond."

"Mr. Artibond. We have a great many things, if you'd care to look."

"No, thanks all the same. Only this morning a fellow was trying to sell me a dog. I was telling Olivia —"

He paused; he had been walking up the stairs beside Lady Evelyn and had glanced over his shoulder, only to see Olivia disappearing round the side of the house with Luis, on her way to the stables. Two more steps and he was in the hall. His eyes, wide and amazed, fixed themselves on the portrait of Lord Quilling.

"Quilling's Cavalry," he said, his tone awed.

"So you know them! I'm so glad to hear that! You haven't seen the trophies before? Then I must show them to you myself. Come along."

Artie did not move.

"Makes you think," he said soberly.

"Makes you think what?" Anabelle asked.

"Well, about that old way of fighting. No protection. Look at them—all exposed up there on their horses, in full view, waving a few feet of sword and charging straight at a pack of beards and turbans. You wouldn't get me doing it, not if you strung four lines of medals across my chest."

"You have to do it before you get the medals," Anabelle pointed out.

"Now this is a most interesting exhibit," Lady Evelyn called. "Come and look."

Reluctantly Artie went to stand beside her.

"That was where three of the most promising young men were assassinated; you can see the terrible scene."

Artie was backing away.

"Crumbs!" he muttered.

"And you can see here the retreat in which so many of them were cut down. My little flags help you to see the place on the map—and here are some sketches of the actual battle."

"Bloodthirsty lot," Artie muttered. "Mind if I get along?"

"In this case, you'll see some souvenirs of the terrible ambush—"

She stopped. Artie, pale green, was at the front door, taking in reviving draughts of air. Without a backward glance, he stumbled down the steps and out of sight.

"An odd young man," Lady Evelyn mused, "but

then, so many of Olivia's friends are odd. Talking of oddities, Anabelle, I heard this morning from old Mrs. Pemberton—Edith Pemberton. She wrote to say that she's giving up her house in Kensington and would let me have some things for the shop if I'd go up on Monday and choose something. You and I might go together; she would give us lunch. Send Luis over here to have lunch with Angus; if it's left to Olivia, she'll feed him on two lettuce leaves. Where is Angus, by the way?"

"I haven't seen him this morning."

"Perhaps he went out. Did you know that he rode with Olivia this morning? A good sign, don't you think? . . . Well, if you want me, I shall be in the kitchen talking to Mrs. Pollard."

She went away. Anabelle went to the room in which she kept her desk, put all other matters firmly from her mind and wrote cheques, brought the account books up to date, and dusted and tidied the room. On her way to the door to go in search of Lady Evelyn, she saw it open; she came face to face with Angus.

He took a quick, impulsive step towards her, but her calm, matter-of-fact greeting halted him.

"Oh Angus, good morning. Your grandmother's been looking for you."

For some moments, frowning, he studied her. She met his gaze steadily, even with faint amusement; if one tried hard enough, she realized, last night could seem a long, long way away.

"What's happened?" he asked.

"I didn't know anything had happened."

"I thought last night had happened—but I may be wrong."

"You were very kind, and I'm very grateful."

"And that's all?"

"For the moment. I'm busy," she pointed out smilingly.

She walked past him; he made no attempt to stop her. She heard his footsteps behind her.

"Anabelle—"

She turned to him.

"Oh, I forgot. Olivia said you were out looking at horses this morning; if you're going back to Mawson's, perhaps you could do something for me."

"Name it."

"You were right about Luis and finance. Fifty pounds arrived by post this morning. Postmark Oporto, but no covering letter. My father suggested spending it on a pony for Luis, so if you could take him along with you and . . . and choose one . . ."

"I'll choose one."

"Thank you."

Once more she turned, but this time he grasped her arm and swung her round towards him. His face was dark with anger.

"Let's hear how you slept," he said.

"Not too well. In fact—"

"In fact, you stayed awake—to think things out. I gave you a night in which to think it over, and so you thought it over. Is that right?"

"Yes. I—"

"And thinking it over, you remembered a lot of things, and by the time morning came you were wondering whether you hadn't let yourself be carried too far too fast. Isn't that true?"

"Yes. Quite true."

"And then—then what? Don't tell me; let me guess. You talked to your father, whose light was on and who probably heard everything that went on. Perhaps he said a word or two. . . . No. He's a man who wisely doesn't speak until he's spoken to. So doubtless he said nothing, and that struck you as ominous. And then—I'm pretty sure that Olivia told you I threw stones to wake her up."

"Yes, she told me."

"Did you believe her?"

"Why shouldn't I believe her?"

"Why? Because truth has two faces. I went away for seven years; when I left, whose room was that? Olivia's? No. It was yours—and so, like a lovesick fool, I got up at dawn and rode across to wake my love. It fell as flat as a novice's dive—but I couldn't tell Olivia that."

He had been gripping her arm. He released it and spoke in a calm, cold voice.

"When you took on Ancell," he said, "you didn't ask for any advice. Knowing what he was, you decided to risk it. Why? I'll tell you why: because taking him on entailed no risk whatsoever; he might be tepid, he might be weak, or spineless, or a bore—but you'd chance it because he'd never give you one moment's anxiety with regard to other women. He was dull, but he was all yours. But loving me—because you did and you do—you lay awake and got carried away by the flood of rumour and lying that bedeviled me all my life in Steyne. I had, you thought, said it all before—so you decided not to risk it. You ignored your poor, fluttering, newly awakened heart and everything it was trying to tell you, and summoned your pride. Well, keep your pride. If I couldn't get through to you last night, it's no use trying any more. I held you in my arms and I told you that I loved you. It was a moment of truth, but you didn't recognize it. You weighed it up, weighed me up—and decided to withdraw. I'm sorry you . . . Oh my God, what's the use of talking?"

He turned and reached the door in three strides. He banged it behind him; she heard his footsteps going across the hall. From the window, she saw him walking towards the stables.

She heard Lady Evelyn calling her. She did not reply. The voice died away and she was left alone in the silence.

Chapter Seven

THROUGHOUT SUNDAY, she and her father were alone. Luis spent the day with Lady Evelyn; Angus took Olivia and Artie on a day-long picnic and they dined at a roadhouse on the way home.

Artie left very early on Monday morning. Anabelle prepared breakfast, had hers with Luis, and then walked with him to the big house. Angus, silent and self-absorbed, drove her and his grandmother to the station to catch the mid-morning train and then went away with Luis.

The journey up to London was accomplished in almost unbroken silence. Anabelle was aware that Lady Evelyn was in a towering temper and guessed that she and Angus had quarreled, but the old lady's only comment on the way was not about Angus but about Philip: Olivia had told her the news and she was very glad to hear it, not to say immensely relieved, and if her advice had been sought in the first place there would have been no engagement, but young people thought they knew everything these days, so what was the use of telling them anything?

There was a long wait for a taxi, and they arrived at Mrs. Pemberton's too late to inspect any of the things before lunch. The meal did nothing to soften Lady Evelyn's mood; the food was poor, the helpings meager, and old Mrs. Pemberton peevish.

After lunch the gifts were displayed and proved to be nothing more than a few pieces of uninteresting china. Lady Evelyn gazed at them in astonishment.

"My dear Edith," she said, "you're surely not going to tell me that you brought me all the way up to London to look at the old nursery china?"

"Take it or leave it," snapped Mrs. Pemberton.

"Do you mean to tell me that in all this great house you've nothing more than this to offer me?"

"I've got daughters and grandchildren; they had first pick."

"I can quite see why they didn't pick this. Eight plates, all cracked—not that that would matter, we sell a great many cracked plates—mugs marked Millicent, Emily, Sophie, and Louisa. I'm surprised at your letting those go; in twenty or thirty years the names might come into fashion again. Jugs without handles —really, Edith, this is a great waste of my time."

"You told me quite distinctly that any old junk would do."

"Not *any* old junk; only *saleable* old junk. I could, for example, sell those cushions and those ornaments and possibly that screen, but I really can't see any sale for Sophie or Louisa."

Edith Pemberton was trembling with rage.

"Mind you, this is your last chance," she warned.

"Last chance to what?" enquired Lady Evelyn.

"If you throw these in my face, it's the last time I donate anything to your shop."

"It's the first time too. Your letter stated quite positively that I could come up and choose. Knowing this house and everything in it so well, I told myself that this was a splendid opportunity for filling the shop. I didn't dream you would confront me with the few pieces of china your children didn't manage to break. Why not hand the things over to your grandchildren?"

"You could have handed them on to your great-grandchildren if you'd known the first thing about handling poor Angus," Mrs. Pemberton brought out venomously. "But all you ever wanted was a dummy cavalryman—to their credit, neither he nor his father would have any of it. Don't think I don't know why he came back to England."

"My dear Edith, you always knew everything about everybody; what you couldn't pry out, you invented. Have you any more cracked china to offer me before I go? Is this all the junk, out of so much junk, that you can spare?"

Mrs. Pemberton, outclassed, could think of nothing to say but good riddance. Lady Evelyn demanded a taxi and drove away with Anabelle; her ill-humour had vanished and she was flushed with triumph. Anabelle had arranged to stay on and do some errands of her own, but the hectic colour on Lady Evelyn's cheeks made her uneasy and she drove to the station with her and remained with her until the train left.

She herself caught one just after four o'clock. It was a fast train; she nearly missed it but sped past a scandalized guard and stepped on as it began to move.

The compartment was empty, but as the train gathered speed she saw a short, dark, very stout man of about fifty walking down the corridor. Looking in, he hesitated and then entered and took a seat in the far corner. He was clearly a foreigner; when he opened his newspaper, Anabelle saw that it was a Portuguese one.

They did not address one another. His presence was enough, however, to bring her mind back to Luis and to the brief, strange meeting with his grandfather. It had now, if possible, an even more unreal quality; the village, the fair, the priest, and the attendant were like figures seen in a dream.

The ticket collector entered and looked at their tickets.

"There is not need to change the train?" the dark man brought out in stumbling English.

"No. No change, sir."

"Thank you."

The sliding door was closed. A friendly glance passed between the man and Anabelle.

"In a strange country, difficulties," he stated.

"I'm sure there are. Are you Portuguese?"

"Yes. You have visited there?"

"I was out there quite recently. I liked it very much."

He bowed. A steward opened the door, offered them tea, and, at the shake of their heads, closed it again. The train slowed, and the man snatched a watch from his pocket and gave an agitated glance at it.

"We're not stopping," Anabelle said. "There's no stop before we get to Steyne."

"To—?"

"Steyne."

"S-t-e-y-n-e?"

"Yes."

He smiled.

"Ah! So that is why there was difficulty at the . . . where I asked for the *billet*."

"Ticket office?"

"Yes. Thank you. I told them I wished to go to Steen. But it is not said like that?"

"No."

There was silence. He took up his paper, seemed to find nothing in it of interest, and put it down again. Glancing at his fellow-passenger, he thought she looked extremely pale; he wondered uneasily if she was one of the people who got ill in trains.

"You wish that I open this window?" he asked.

"Please. It's . . . it's rather warm."

It was time, she told herself fiercely, to get over this lunatic idea that Portugal was simply Luis. Just because she happened to run into a Portuguese who happened to be going to Steyne . . ..

But why would he be going to Steyne? Steyne was a small, sparsely populated seaside town. It had no beaches. It had no season and no attractions for tourists. It had no large firms, no factories; it had two small and unpretentious hotels. It had, or was close to, a large school, but the school was served by St. Thomas's station, and anybody going there would have taken a slow train and changed to the branch line.

"Are you"—she found herself speaking and was

surprised, for she had determined to say nothing—
"are you staying in England long?"

"Long? Oh, no, no, no. A few days only."

A pause. This time it was he who spoke.

"You live there, in Steyne?"

"Yes. I hope you'll enjoy your stay there."

"Stay? Oh, but as you see"—he waved a hand towards the luggage rack, where nothing of his reposed
but a small black brief case—"I come, I go away. It is
only business about a little boy; no more."

She kept her eyes on the scenery that had begun to
swirl strangely outside the window. A small boy. If
the small boy was Luis, if the man seated opposite
was the first indication that Luis's visit was to end—
then he must know her name. If he had come
legitimately . . .

Her heart was beating fast. Opposition. There had
been—Luis's grandfather had said—grave opposition.
Nobody had prevented Luis from coming to England,
but those who had opposed his coming could have
found out where he was, could have followed him.
Her mind went back to the *Yeoman* and she remembered that Angus had spoken to Luis and that Luis
had spoken of an uncle. The uncle had been called
Alberto—no, Alfredo. Luis had not liked him—and
he was fat; very fat. . . .

She stared across at her companion. His eyes were
closed. He looked even less attractive in sleep than he
had done awake. Small and stout and far from prepossessing. Not the man, she was convinced, to have been
chosen by Luis's grandfather to bring back his grandson.

She would not mention Luis's name—but if this
man had come from Senhor Ribeiro he would surely
know who she was. He would have a message for her,
or a letter; of so much she could be certain. It was
impossible for him to be going to Steyne on an honest
errand unless it had some connection with herself.

The train swayed and he opened his eyes. She decided that she could not reasonably demand his name
—but she would tell him hers and await his reactions.

She spoke slowly and clearly.

"I am Anabelle Baird," she said.

It was obvious that it meant nothing at all. He showed an instant of mild astonishment and then gave a rather embarrassed bow.

The slowing of the train came to her rescue. She looked out. They were passing the village of Outersteyne; they were almost at Steyne itself. He would get out and go in search of Luis. . . .

Suddenly, desperately, she wanted to see Angus. Angus would know what to do. Angus could deal with this. Miracles did happen; perhaps he would be on the platform waiting. . . .

He was not on the platform. So much a glance up and down told her as the train drew slowly in. What happened next, happened without any conscious plan on her part. It just, she was to protest later, over and over again, it just happened.

She was standing up. The train stopped and she opened the door. The man had risen. She turned and addressed him smilingly.

"Didn't you say you wanted Steyne?"

"Yes. But this—"

He craned his neck, but she was blocking the view.

"Oh no. There are two Steynes, you see." So much, at any rate, was true. "This is only the station for Upper Steyne."

And that was true too. And so was the sound of the whistle.

"You get out at the next stop," she told him.

He sat down again. She was out and had swung the door closed and was standing back to watch the train gather speed. The next stop, she knew well, was in an hour and a half, and he would get out and find himself in Somerset; and her father, who had absently done the same thing more than once, could tell him that getting back to Steyne was a slow and tortuous business.

He would go back to London. He would come again but not today. Perhaps tomorrow—and by tomorrow she would have told Angus what had happened. All she had to do was find Angus.

She ignored the signals from the taxi drivers outside

the station. She wanted to walk; she needed air. She took the road to the sea and walked with the wind in her face, along the wide sea road and then along the steep narrow path that would lead her up through rocks and boulders to her home. But she would not go home; she would cut through to the big house and find Angus.

She paused for breath. The wind here was stronger; she was halfway between the level of the lower line of houses and the larger, more widely separated ones that stood on the hill. She could see, high up, the chimneys of the big house; she could see the buildings which had once belonged to it and which Angus's grandfather had sold: the laundry, the coach house, the east lodge.

She took the remainder of the climb in long, easy strides. Soon she was hurrying along the wooded path that led to Lady Evelyn's.

There were lights in the drawing room; she entered by one of the long windows. Lady Evelyn, clearly restored to good humour, turned to greet her.

"Come in, Anabelle, my dear; so you got back safely."

"Yes. Where's Angus?"

The reason for the good humour became clear.

"Angus? You'll never guess."

"Where?"

"He drove off with Olivia to a roadhouse that's opening tonight. There's a sort of gala dinner, and dancing afterwards. I don't expect him back early. I think things are really going well. Anabelle, you look tired; why not stay and have a little light dinner with me?"

"No, thank you. I must get home."

She turned and went out and closed the window carefully behind her. She walked slowly homewards and felt the tears trickling down her cheeks. Perhaps Lady Evelyn was right; perhaps things were going well.

But not for her . . .

Chapter Eight

SHE WAS IN Olivia's room early the following morning, leaning over the bed and shaking her gently awake. Olivia stirred and murmured sleepily.

"Time?"

"It's early—only ten to eight. I brought you a cup of tea. I'm sorry to start talking so early—I know you were late home—but I had to see you."

Olivia sat up and waved the tea aside.

"I'll go down and get some coffee. What's the panic?"

"No panic." That, for a start, was a lie; a slip of the tongue. "I just wanted to know something about that dog that Artie said he was offered."

"*Dog?*"

"Yes."

"What do you want to know about the dog for?"

"I want to buy one."

"Buy one?"

"Yes."

"A dog?" Olivia was fully awake. "Why a dog suddenly?"

"I was thinking about it during the night. Artie said it was a watchdog."

"Did you hear burglars or something?"

"No. I—"

"Philip been trying to climb through your window and rape you?"

"As far as I know, Philip is in Lisbon. I rang up the pub Artie stayed at, and they remember the dog but they don't remember the man. Did Artie see him again?"

"Look, are you—"

"Olivia, this is important. I didn't come in here and wake you up just to clear up your doubts as to whether I'm crazy or not crazy; all I'd like to know is: did Artie meet the man again? Just say yes or no and leave the comment for another time."

"Yes, he did."

"Where?"

"He came up to us on Sunday evening, when Angus and I dropped Artie at the pub after dinner. If you're after a dog, you can't go after that one. It's as big as a camel, and it puts the fear of God into everybody who looks at it."

"Did the man give any address?"

"He said he wanted to get rid of the dog because he lived in a caravan. Artie says he must have stolen the dog, because nobody in their senses would have tried to get an animal that size into anything smaller than a hangar."

Caravan. There was no caravan site nearer than the camp some miles beyond St. Thomas's College. But Mr. Mawson sometimes let out his field. . . .

"Did you see a caravan when you were at Mawson's on Saturday?"

"No. I can't say I did."

"Thanks. Shall I make your coffee, or are you going to sleep again?"

"I'm going down; I may as well."

"Luis is having his breakfast; I'm taking him to school."

"I thought he took himself to school."

"I'm going to try and find this man with the dog—on the way."

"You wouldn't care to explain or anything?"

"Later."

Luis was willing enough to set out early in order to look at a dog which sounded as extraordinary as this one. He watched Anabelle as she backed her father's

car out of the garage, and then clambered in beside
her.

She drove to Mawson's, but she drove without hope;
if there had been a caravan there, Olivia would have
seen it. There was no permanent caravan site; owners
were permitted a stay of two days only. Perhaps the
man with the dog had gone.

There was no caravan on Mr. Mawson's land—but
he might know something. It was worth asking.

Mr. Mawson, like herself, had been up and about
since dawn.

"Chap came and asked me if he could park in my
fields, but I didn't like the look of him. And he had a
dog that looked dangerous."

"Have you any idea where he went?"

"I advised him to try the caravan site, but he said it
was full. I told him the only other hope was the field
over at Dancy's, if Dancy would let him have it."

Mr. Dancy was the town's dentist. He was not yet
up—but clearly visible at the edge of his property was
a small, battered-looking caravan.

The man who came to its door to watch the car approaching was unshaven and seedy and looked as
though he had slept in his clothes. His eyes were
shifty and his expression was sly, and Anabelle realized as soon as she had stopped the car and stepped
out that it would have been wiser to have let him
come to her. It would also have been cheaper; even as
she explained what had brought her, his manner was
changing from shiftiness to smugness.

"You couldn't," he told her in a hoarse, falsely jovial voice, "have come to a better place."

"You haven't sold the dog?"

"Could 'a done; could 'a done more than once,
lady. But I'd got fond of 'im, see? I didn't want ter let
'im go ter the first comer what gimme me price. A
good 'ome, that was the main thing; a good 'ome for a
good dog. 'E's always been used to kindness, and I
didn't see m'self letting 'im go to somebody 'oo only
wanted 'im to eat burglars. Affection, I said; that was
the—"

"Could you show me the dog? Is it here?"

He smiled an odious smile.

"Lady, if I kept that dog in that caravan, I'd 'ave ter sleep outside. What's more, Mr. Dentist Dancy agreed to rent me this field, but 'e said I'd 'ave ter lock the dog up. Frightened out of 'is pants, 'e was, and I don't wonder. The—"

"Will you let me see the dog, please?"

"Cer-tainly, lady; cer-tainly. I'm not sure even now if I'll sell 'im, but you can cer-tainly take a look."

He led the way; Anabelle followed with Luis. They walked towards the stables, which she knew to be occupied not by horses but by Mr. Dancy's Angora rabbits.

The rabbits were in the first loose-box. Luis, after one look, separated himself from the party and stood fascinated before the large, well-kept hutches. Anabelle went on with the man to the last stall. He opened the top half of the door and stood aside.

Anabelle looked in—and felt her heart in her mouth.

She was looking at an animal which, even in the gloom of the stable, looked so forbidding that she felt she would never have the courage, even if she came to terms with its unsavoury owner, to lead it out to the car.

It was almost as large as Artie had claimed. It was shaggy. Its eyes peered out through a tangle of long hair. It was black and white, with a head that was like a baby calf's. Its origins were obscure.

The owner was making hoarse, wheedling noises.

"Good dog; good ole dog; how's the ole dog, then?"

The dog, standing on its bed of straw, made no move. Anabelle put out a hand—and heard the animal give a sudden terrifying sound, half growl, half ship's siren. She drew her hand hastily back. The dog sprang forward, straining on its chain, its body hurled again and again towards the door.

"Dangerous," pointed out the man. "But what d'you need in a watchdog, after all? If you want ter frighten people, you want to frighten 'em—and that dog does."

"How much?"

"For you, a price as low as I'd dare ask, consid'ring all 'e's cost me in feed. I can see you'd give 'im a good—"

"How much are you asking for him?"

"Ten pounds, lady."

"Then why did you tell a friend of mine that you only wanted three?"

"Three? *Three!* Three pounds for that—"

"All right, I'll give you four—if you'll lead him to my car and see him safely in."

"Four pounds? Why, it's—"

"I won't pay more. I shouldn't pay you more than three, but I'm in a hurry. Hurry or not, if you don't agree to four pounds, there's no deal." And there went the last of the fifty pounds from Portugal.

There was something in her voice that carried conviction.

"Four pounds; very well, lady. It's robbery, but I told you before; a good 'ome's all I'm asking. If you—"

He stopped. Anabelle had lunged past him—but she was too late. While they had been bargaining, Luis had stopped looking at rabbits and had come to look at the dog. Since he could not see over the lower half of the door, he had, before anybody could stop him, lifted its latch and stepped inside.

"Luis!" screamed Anabelle.

She managed to push the man out of the way—but even as she did so, even as she leapt through the open doorway, she knew that there was no need to hurry, or to worry. Luis needed help, but not of the kind she had envisaged. He was being half devoured—but the growling, the howling, the short deep barks were far from threatening. The great tongue was licking any part of Luis that it could reach. The vast paws had sent the boy reeling against the door, but if ever Anabelle had seen ecstatic joy, welcoming love in an animal, she was seeing it again now.

She heard, through a haze of relief, the man's voice.

"See what I mean? Dangerous—except when 'e

knows 'e belongs ter yer. Intelligent as they come; 'e knew I'd found a good 'ome for him."

Anabelle did not bother to reply. She was opening her bag and taking out the money. She was completely certain that the dog had been stolen; the man had probably been brought up short by the sight of him and had discovered that the fierce front was misleading. He may have stolen it to guard his caravan— or merely to sell to a credulous client.

Stolen or not, the dog was for the time being hers. She was submitting to overtures scarcely less overwhelming than those which had greeted Luis. There was no need to ask the man's assistance in getting the dog to the car; released, he frisked awkwardly between Anabelle and Luis and bounded past them to smell out trees and bushes, circling with a wild delight that told her he had been too long in captivity.

She heard the man telling her that the dog's name was Cocktail. Discarding it, she turned to Luis.

"What would you say his name was?" she asked.

"I can give him a name?"

"Yes. What's it to be?"

"Foguete." The choice was unhesitating.

"Foo-get?"

"Foguete, yes."

"It means . . ." She paused. "I know. It's the name of the fast train that runs between Lisbon and Oporto, and it means rocket. All right; Foguete he is."

She thought the name unsuitable, but she did not care much and the dog cared not at all. He was doing his best to get into the car at the same time as Luis; at Luis's shrill protest, he tumbled in a huge heap from the step and rose to butt the boy in before scrambling in after him. He spilled over onto the driving seat, and it took all Anabelle's strength and persuasiveness to bundle him, with Luis's help, into the back. He sat there with his head towering between them, his tongue hanging out, his breath fanning their hair. Anabelle put the car into gear and then held the chain out to the dog's late owner.

"Keep it," she said. "We won't need it."

She drove towards the school, happier than she had been since getting off the train the day before. She thought of asking Mrs. Swann not to allow Luis to leave the school before she came to fetch him and rejected the idea; there would be questions, and she could not answer them.

Getting Luis out and keeping Foguete in took time and skill. His previous owner—legitimate owner—had doubtless been a boy, Anabelle decided; having failed to squeeze himself through the open window in pursuit of Luis, he hung out his head and howled. Children screamed, escorting parents or guardians snatched up their charges, and Mrs. Swann, appearing framed in the doorway as Anabelle drove away, stood transfixed. There were going to be drawbacks, it was clear, to dog-keeping on this scale.

Halfway home, Foguete stopped howling and licked Anabelle's cheek to indicate that he liked her a little too. The caress left her face feeling as though the skin had been scraped off.

He knew a home when he saw one. He did not wait for the door on his side to be opened; the moment the driving seat was empty, he hurled himself out, rolled over three times, and began a dance of delight. He went round and round the trees, took the corner of the house on two legs and knocked over the dustbin, lifted his leg and drowned half a flower bed, tried to leap over the car. Then he charged the holly hedge; this was a mistake, and he was the first to admit it.

Throughout, Anabelle stood with her back against a tree; if that vast body leapt at her, it would send her headlong. She saw her father's face at his window. Olivia opened the kitchen door, gave a yell, and banged it just in time to intercept Foguete's friendly rush. Mr. Baird opened the upper window and threw out a strap which Anabelle recognized as the one that had secured her school trunk; she joined the two ends, managed to lasso the dog, and tightened the strap round his neck. He sat down and panted.

"Listen, you," she said. "You'll exercise down by the sea or in the woods—but not in this garden."

Olivia was approaching cautiously. Presently Mr. Baird came out; they stood looking at the dog, who looked up at them lovingly; when his feelings became too much for him, he gave a low, tremulous, emotion-charged growl.

"You're not going to leave him here when you go to Lady Evelyn's, are you?" her father asked anxiously.

"No. I'll take him."

"He'll take you," Olivia said.

"Hold him, will you?" Anabelle asked. "I'll get him some water."

"You hold him; I'll get the water."

She brought it in the small enamel bowl which served as a bird bath; he drank it in four great laps, picked up the basin in his teeth and pushed it against her.

"Well, he talks!" Olivia said admiringly. When she came out with a second helping, it was in a bucket; for a long time there was no sound but that of splashing. The water level dropped and dropped, and at last Foguete was full.

"About three pounds of meat a day, I'd say," Mr. Baird said reflectively.

Anabelle met his eyes and saw in them a look of understanding. She had been ashamed of her action on the train, and she had said nothing to him of the incident. She was also ashamed of her impulsive action in buying a dog—but her father knew why she had done so; he might not approve, but at least he could understand and perhaps sympathize. . . .

She took Foguete with her when she went to work, letting him run free; on Pemberton land she felt that they were safe from trespassers. She threw the dog twigs and small stones to encourage him to tire himself out, and wondered what Angus would say when he saw her purchase—and when she told him of yesterday's meeting on the train.

She went round to the stables and tied Foguete securely; beside him she put the steak that was to have been their dinner and the bones that were to have made their soup. She patted his head and promised to come back for him; not until she was almost out of sight did he give his attention to the food.

She walked swiftly towards the house; Angus's horses were in the stables, so that there was every reason to hope that she could see him before he went out. Her spirits rose; she was badly in need of advice, and he was he only one who could supply it.

She entered the house. Crossing the hall, she walked down a corridor and looked into the dining room; it was empty and there was no place laid at the table. Hearing footsteps, she turned and saw Lady Evelyn coming towards her.

"Good morning, Lady Evelyn. I was looking to see if Angus was here."

The old lady came closer, and she saw on her face signs of anger and excitement.

"Angus," she said in a high, sharp voice, "has gone up to London. He won't be back until tomorrow."

Anabelle's heart sank—but the tone in which Lady Evelyn had spoken did not encourage questions. There was nothing to do but follow her to the shop and begin the morning's work.

It soon became clear that it was not one of Lady Evelyn's good days. Something had upset her. When upset, she would usually sulk for an hour and then break into bitter but vague accusations; finally she would come to the point and state her grievances. She and Angus had obviously quarreled and he had gone. . . .

At the thought of his going and not returning, Anabelle grew cold with fear. There was desolation too, but at this moment fear predominated. He was the only one she could turn to in her problems concerning Luis. There was no one else. He had been in it—no, not in it, but he had known of it—from the beginning. He had shown no desire to involve himself too deeply, but he had at least been there, a support if she needed one.

"I wish," Lady Evelyn burst out at last, "that people would make up their minds what to do with their lives and do it. A man of twenty-two is old enough, surely, to stick to his decisions. But no. Having gone away for ever, Angus decides that here, after all, is where he wants to be. He went away and left me to run this great place alone. He deserted me—an old widow, and a childless widow at that, and went thousands of miles away and lived among foreigners, and then what does he do? He—are you listening to what I'm saying?"

"I'm listening."

"Then you might make some kind of comment."

"Isn't this between Angus and yourself?"

"Does that mean that nobody else can offer an opinion?"

"If you feel worried, why don't you go across and talk to my father?"

"I am not in the least worried. I am merely angry. Since Angus came back, I haven't known one moment's peace. I will not be bullied. I have a right to do as I please with my own. To hear him, one would imagine that I was going to leave him homeless and penniless. If I left this house to him, he would sell it at once."

"No, he wouldn't."

"He told me quite categorically when he went to Brazil—"

"That was seven years ago. He's changed."

Lady Evelyn stared angrily at her.

"Are you on his side? As far as I know, you never liked him."

Anabelle met the stormy gaze.

"Did you?" she asked.

"Did I what?"

"Did you ever . . . like him?"

Two red spots—signs of her most towering wrath —appeared on Lady Evelyn's cheeks.

"That is extremely impertinent," she said.

"Perhaps it is. But you asked for my comments, and seeing you two together lately I've found myself wondering . . . or perhaps I understand him better than I did when I was younger. As long as I've known you both, you've wanted one thing and he's wanted another. I used to think that you were quite right and he was quite wrong, but now I know that he had a lot of right on his side. But even if he wasn't much of a grandson before he went to Brazil, he's come back prepared to—"

"You mean that after seven years alone, seven years in which he gave no sign of ever wanting to see me or to see this place again, I must receive him with open arms, change my plans, change the decisions I made with regard to my own house and my own money? Is that what you mean?"

"I suppose it is. Lately I've thought about you; I've tried to see this from your point of view; I've tried to put myself into . . . into your shoes. But once I step into them I don't see any problem, because the whole thing seems to me to come down to one single fact."

"Which is?"

Anabelle's voice was gentle.

"The fact that he's all you've got. Apart from you, he's got nobody. Apart from him, you've got nobody. And he didn't go away; you sent him away."

"And I wish, I only wish he'd stayed away. It wasn't affection that brought him home; it was greed. Greed—and fear that he was going to lose something. He came home to see what I had in mind. What I had in mind is only what I've had in mind for years—a memorial to my grandfather. I want this house to be a rallying place for the descendants of those men who fought for our Empire when we had an Empire. This morning I told Angus that nothing he could say or do would make any difference; I would sign the new will. And then he threatened me."

"Threatened?"

"What else but threatened? He said that he knew one sure way of stopping me and he would use it. I told him that the only course for him was to go back to Brazil and he . . . he laughed. He said that if I signed, that's just what he would do—but he didn't think I would sign. He walked out of the room saying that he was going up to London and he would be back tomorrow, and that there would be no signing. Is that threatening or isn't it? Why should he bully me?"

There was a pause.

"Perhaps it's his turn," Anabelle suggested quietly.

"I don't understand you."

"You bullied him for twenty-two years. You tried to drill him; you tried to make him see Quilling's Cavalry as you saw it. You wanted him to grow up in your grandfather's image; you were, in fact, determined that he should grow up in your grandfather's image. You tried to compel him—coerce him. You bullied him."

Her eyes were on her desk. When she raised them it was to see, to her horror, two slow tears trickling down the old lady's cheeks.

She had never in her life seen her cry. In an instant she was beside her, cradling her in her arms.

"Lady Evelyn, please . . . *please!* You shouldn't have . . . I shouldn't have. . . ."

She helped her to unfold the small square of linen and dab the quivering cheeks. Then Lady Evelyn freed herself and walked to the window, and stood there staring out at the evenly planted rows of trees.

"If he'd been like Luis," she said quaveringly, "I could have loved him."

There was nothing to say. It was useless to point out that Luis provided her with the little toy soldier she had longed all her life to play with. The very set of Luis's head must have set her feet marching in the old, heady rhythm. Death had taken her son; she had sent her grandson away.

"This morning"—Lady Evelyn dried her tears and spoke on the same tremulous note—"he had a telephone call. It was put through to me by mistake, so I knew that it was a London call. I guessed it must be from Mr. Sanders—they've been in touch ever since Angus came home. Then Angus came to my room and we . . . we quarreled. Can you blame me for feeling upset? Can you—?"

She stopped; something about Anabelle seemed to have caught her attention. After studying her for some moments, she walked slowly over to stand beside the desk. When she spoke, her tone was gentle.

"I'm a selfish old woman," she said. "You're looking worn out. I ought to have remembered that even if others can't regret your broken engagement, you must be feeling upset. You told me no details—perhaps you don't care to talk about it?"

"Philip came home to talk about the date of the wedding. He—"

"He wanted to put if off *again?*"

"No. Put it on. I told him it was impossible; I couldn't have left Luis."

"Well, you know that you could have sent the boy to me; you must have realized that, after you, there is nobody he is more fond of than myself. I would have been only too happy to have kept him here with me until he went back to Portugal—but why were you to advance the wedding date?"

Anabelle did not reply; she had glanced at her watch and was hastily putting away papers.

"It's nearly half-past twelve," she said. "I've got to fetch Luis."

"My watch was perfectly correct by the wireless this morning. It's just ten past," Lady Evelyn said.

Anabelle put the hands of her watch back but closed her desk.

"I wish I'd had daughters," Lady Evelyn said wistfully. "It would have been so much more companionable. I could have been of some use, some help to daughters—perhaps."

Anabelle, glad to see her embarked upon daughters instead of grandsons, listened in silence. When she left, Lady Evelyn accompanied her to the door and patted her cheek.

"I must look for a husband for you," she said. "You would have been wasted on Philip Ancell."

Anabelle left her and ran down the steps and turned towards the stables. Foguete saw her before she saw him; his wild baying broke out and echoed in the hills and made the horses snort.

She led him through the wood and felt relieved when they were out of sight of the house. She would have to show her purchase to Lady Evelyn, but there had been no opportunity, today, to talk of dogs. She would . . .

She halted. Far away, but umistakable, was Luis's

figure. He was making his way across to the Coach House, taking the short cut through Pemberton property. He must, she thought, have left early—and then she glanced at her watch and the reason for his appearance became clear. Her watch had been correct —but Lady Evelyn, absorbed in the fascinating topic of the engagement, had been unwilling to let her go. *My watch was perfectly correct....*

A slip of the tongue. It was a long time since she had been caught; it would be, resolved Anabelle, a long time before she allowed herself to be caught again. But all was well; Luis was near, and all she had to do was let Foguete free . . . but that would be unwise; he would knock Luis off his feet.

It was Foguete who saw the second figure. He had been straining at the strap, and his sudden immobility made her wonder what he had seen. And then she too saw.

Short and stout . . . and hastening after Luis. She could not be mistaken. The man was stumbling over the rough ground, his eyes on the boy, his intention plainly to overtake him.

She realized that she was screened from the house, from Luis, from the stranger. As she stood hesitating for a brief moment, Luis broke into the one-two-three-skip he often adopted as a cross between walking and running. The distance between him and the man increased—and then Anabelle moved. With a low, inarticulate sound that communicated to the dog something of her fear, she streaked in a direct line towards the trespasser.

He turned and uttered a cry of terror. She was almost upon him; beside her the great dog was surging forward, his panting breath sounding like a repeated threat.

The stranger, with a wild look to left and right, displayed an agility Anabelle would not have expected from one of his bulk. He chose his tree and was up it, clinging, at the same moment that she came to a halt.

He had obtained a precarious foothold on one of the lower branches. His arms round another, he was staring down at her, his eyes starting with fright. She addressed him in clear tones.

"You may come down," she said. "I shall hold this dog until you are outside the gates. If you hesitate or turn back, I shall let him loose."

He did not speak; if he had tried to utter a sound, she thought that he would not have succeeded. He slid slowly and painfully down from among the branches, his eyes on the dog straining at the leash.

He walked rapidly away, first with his head turned to keep the dog in sight, and then in desperate haste to the gates and so out into the road. With a last brief backward glance he was gone.

She stood where she was, her hand on the dog's coat, caressing him absently.

"Good dog. . . . Good Foguete. . . ."

She turned to follow Luis homeward. As she moved away from the tree, something she thought was a branch came sliding down and fell at her feet. It was Foguete who picked it up delicately between his teeth and let her take it from him.

It was a small black brief case. She had seen it once before: yesterday, on the luggage rack above the Portuguese stranger's head.

She took it to her father. The case was locked, but even if it had not been she would not have been able to bring herself to examine its contents. She laid it on the table at which her father was seated at work.

"Trouble," she said.

Pulling up a chair, she sat down and related the story briefly, beginning at the moment the Portuguese entered the train. When she had finished, her father sat gazing at the small black case; he had made no move to pick it up.

"I'm not strong on law," he said musingly. "Old Sanders would be useful now. Sending that fellow on in the train would come under misrepresentation, I daresay; sending him up a tree . . . well, there was no actual assault, was there?"

"His clothes were torn."

"I suppose this brief case ought to go to the police."

"If Angus had been here, it wouldn't have happened. He would have caught the man and made him talk. But he wasn't here."

"He'll be back tomorrow, you said?"

"Yes."

"Then we'll wait until he gets back and see what he advises. I'd rather he dealt with the police."

"Does it have to be the police?"

"How else will the man recover his property? To look inside for his name and address would mean breaking open the lock, and I don't care to do that. I'm sorry that something like this happened—but why did you rush to the conclusion that it was a wicked uncle coming to abduct his nephew?"

"I told you. He—"

"He was coming openly, and he was coming with some kind of papers."

"If he had come from Luis's grandfather, he *must* have been told my name. Luis's grandfather knew it. Father Vicento knew it. How could they trust me with Luis and then allow somebody to come for him without telling them who I was? I always knew that Luis would have to go—some day—but I'm absolutely certain that this wouldn't have been the way his grandfather would have taken him away."

Mr. Baird began to speak and then appeared to think better of it.

"I know what you want to say. You want to say that this is the beginning of the end."

"Something like that," he admitted. "Whoever the man is, I think you must—"

"I'm not the only one who's going to miss him. How about Lady Evelyn? If it comes to that, how about you?"

"I like the boy. Who wouldn't? But for you it's going to be hard."

"Well, it hasn't happened yet."

Her father picked up the case.

"And this must be given to Angus."

"Will you keep it until tomorrow?"

"Very well."

She went downstairs; Olivia was preparing to serve lunch. Luis was persuaded to come indoors to eat his and then ran out again to join Foguete. Mr. Baird went upstairs and Anabelle cleared the dining room and began to wash up. Olivia dried the spoons and forks, polished the knives and the glasses, and then levered herself up onto the table and sat with her legs swinging.

"You going back to the big house?" she asked Anabelle.

"Not today. Why?"

"You could have told Lady Evelyn that her scheme misfired."

"What scheme?"

"Joining Angus and myself in holy matrimony. What I can't understand is how you've put up with her all these years. She's spoiled, she's selfish, and she's stupid."

"I know."

"If you know, why have you stayed stuck down here working for her?"

"One reason was that I didn't want to live in London."

"You needn't have stayed there—but you should have got away from here. If you had, you would have learned to . . . well, how can I put it? This way: Clare and I have learned what we want; you haven't. We got out of a small pool into the big rough sea and learned how to swim. You didn't. She and I scratched up some kind of design for living—but you? You waste your life working for a bullying old bitch, you nearly get married to a jellyfish—and when a prize like Angus comes along, you let him go."

"Did Angus tell you that?"

"What do you think we did last night—dance? No. We talked—about you. Why did you tie yourself into knots and end up by convincing yourself he was a rake? You got scared, didn't you?"

"Yes, I did."

"Why? Because after he'd kissed you he didn't say: I love you, I have your father's consent and your sisters' approval, will you please marry me at St. Something's at three o'clock on the afternoon of Saturday the fourth of June? Good heavens, Anabelle, a man like Angus tells you he loves you, tells you he wants you, and . . . For Pete's sake, what century are you living in? Do you think men like that come again and again, nosegay in fist, waiting for you to come out of your scare? Do you?"

"No."

"Then why did you act that way with Angus? If he'd given me a birdseed of encouragement I'd have gone for him myself—but he didn't want me; he wanted you. And all you can think of is how many women he's chased in the past. Don't you realize that any woman who can catch more than one look from a man as attractive—and as choosey—as Angus, goes about claiming to have slept with him? He's a success symbol. One admiring word from him, and you can pin on a rosette. You can . . . Here, where are you going?"

"Up to my room."

"What for?"

"To howl."

"Have you listened to one single word I've been saying?"

"Yes. But—"

"Yes but what?"

"I wish you'd said it long ago, that's all."

Chapter Nine

ON THE FOLLOWING AFTERNOON, Luis and Anabelle agreed, after consulting together, that it was time to introduce Foguete to Lady Evelyn. They walked over together to the big house; Lady Evelyn, coming out onto the terrace as they approached, looked at the dog in disbelief, gave a loud cry, and leveled her stick in its direction.

"Keep it away!" she called. "If you let it come near me, I shall attack it with my stick. What kind of animal is it?"

Luis, rolling on the ground with laughter, got up to explain that it was a dog, a tame dog, his dog, a watchdog.

"He will only push you over," he said. "He will not bite you. He likes you—see, he is trying to go to you."

"I can see that. Tell him to keep his distance. I don't believe it's a dog at all. Take him away, Anabelle, and leave Luis with me."

"I will take him to the stables," Luis said. "He can stay there. Then we shall do some left-right, left-right?"

"Yes," Lady Evelyn promised.

He led, or was led by, Foguete along the graveled path leading to the stables. Anabelle walked with Lady Evelyn along the terrace.

"Come indoors for a moment, Anabelle; it's too warm in the sun. Has your father seen that monstrous dog?"

"Yes."

"Then he must have pointed out the cost of feeding it. What on earth made you buy it—or was it given to you?"

"I bought it. For . . . for Luis."

It was in one sense true. True or not, she saw at once that since it was for Luis, Lady Evelyn had nothing more to say against it.

"Come and sit by the window," she invited. "Luis will be back presently and then he and I must look through some of those old photographs in my grandfather's albums. He was rather taken with the sketches of the camels; no, I told him, they weren't for riding but for carrying loads. He—"

She broke off, a little annoyed; Anabelle was not attending. She was standing at the window staring out.

"Anabelle—"

Once more she broke off, this time from uneasiness. Anabelle's face was ashen, her eyes wide with apprehension.

A terrible picture of Luis lying out there, injured or worse, brought the old lady to her feet and to the window at a swift, stumbling pace. Gazing out, she saw nothing unusual: the terrace, the short stretch of lawn, the woods beyond; all seemed empty.

"Luis—" she began in alarm.

Anabelle glanced at her.

"No, not Luis."

"Then what is it? You gave me a dreadful fright; I thought something had happened to him. I do wish you—"

This time the words trailed off. Anabelle's mind was not on her. She waited a few moments and then touched her on the shoulder.

"Anabelle, my eyes are not what they were. If there's something or someone out there, remember that this is my property and that I have a right to be informed. What are you staring at?"

"A man."

"A man? If somebody has come and wants to see me, he'll come up to the house—or go round to the other side of the house. Who is he?"

"A man I met on the train coming back from London. A Portuguese."

She spoke mechanically; she was talking more to herself than to Lady Evelyn. Her eyes fixed on the short, stout form outside, she scarcely realized what she was saying.

"You met him on the train? He annoyed you?"

"He frightened me. I thought he'd come to . . . to take Luis away."

Lady Evelyn stared at the white, tense profile and then sank slowly onto the window seat. Never a slow thinker, and at all times disposed to jump to erroneous conclusions, she now had no hesitation in building her own construction on the evidence before her. Luis, whose presence nobody had really explained satisfactorily. Luis, who carried himself like a princeling. Luis . . .

Anabelle was speaking in the same sleepwalker tone.

"I bought the dog because I was frightened. If Angus had been here . . . but he wasn't. Yesterday I saw the man. He was following Luis. Luis ran ahead, but I was there—with the dog. I threatened the man and he took refuge up a tree and I stood there until he had left the grounds. But he lost a brief case; it fell down from the tree after he'd left, and I should have known that he'd come back for it. And that's what he's doing out there now—looking for the case. He—"

"Where is this brief case?"

Anabelle turned, and her eyes lost something of their blank look.

"At home. I took it to my father, and he said I was to give it to Angus, who'd give it to the police."

Lady Evelyn rose. She seemed to rise a long way, and Anabelle realized that during those moments in which she had been staring out the window she had spoken her thoughts aloud—and said far too much.

"Ring that bell," commanded Lady Evelyn.

She was standing with her head held high, one hand on the knob of her stick. Seized with dismay at the thought of interference, Anabelle hesitated.

"Ring that bell," Lady Evelyn repeated.

Anabelle rang it. In the interval before it was answered, Lady Evelyn stood unmoving, her eyes on the door. When it opened, she addressed the woman on the threshold in authoritative accents.

"Mrs. Pollock, there is a man outside in the woods; you can see him from this window. Will you kindly go and tell him that I wish to speak to him?"

"But—" began Anabelle and fell silent as Lady Evelyn, without glancing in her direction, raised a thin, peremptory hand.

"Just say that and nothing more, Mrs. Pollock: Lady Evelyn Pemberton wishes to see him. Don't parley with him; bring him to me."

Mrs. Pollock closed the door. Anabelle would have liked to speak, but Lady Evelyn motioned her to a chair and then stood with her eyes fixed expectantly on the door.

"I am surprised," she said severely, "that you went so far as to deal with trespassers on my grounds without a word to me. I would have thought that you, better than anybody, would know how fond I have grown of Luis; anything concerning his welfare could safely have been entrusted to me. You took quite the wrong line with this man; I shall stand no nonsense, I assure you, from anybody, Portuguese or not, who wishes to interfere with Luis."

Footsteps sounded outside the door. Lady Evelyn walked slowly forward and took up a position in the middle of the room. Anabelle rose to her feet and found that her knees were shaking.

The door had opened. Mrs. Pollock ushered in a stout form, murmured something unintelligible, and withdrew.

There had been a frown on his face when he entered—but as his eyes fell on Anabelle, it darkened to a look of rage. Taking a step in her direction, and ignoring Lady Evelyn—which was a mistake—he spoke in a thick, furious voice.

"So it is you!" he said. "I have—"

"Stop!" commanded Lady Evelyn. "I do not know your name, but I should like to say that you have seriously annoyed my friend, Miss Baird. You have done more: you have trespassed on my property. You will kindly remain here while I telephone to the police."

Anabelle's heart sank; she had indeed said far too much. How, knowing Lady Evelyn as she did, she could have allowed herself to . . . But it was too late, she realized, for regrets. These were the deep waters of which Angus had spoken.

The man had turned to Lady Evelyn, his face growing pale.

"The police!"

He gave a hunted look round the room; he looked like a man on the verge of flight.

"Stay where you are!" warned Lady Evelyn. "You will remain here until the police come, and you can then give an account of yourself. Anabelle, you will please go and telephone to Inspector Reed and ask him to send a constable over at once. I shall keep this man here in the meantime."

The stranger's face, during this speech, had been a study in concentration; his face was screwed up, one ear was inclined in the speaker's direction in an effort to follow all that was being said. How much he had understood, Anabelle did not know, but as Lady Evelyn finished speaking, he walked towards her with his arms upraised.

"No!" he shouted. "Certainly no! No police!"

"Anabelle, you heard me," said Lady Evelyn implacably.

The man hesitated, gazed wildly round—and then turned towards the door. Lady Evelyn's warning voice rang out.

"Stop!"

His hand was on the latch. Without the slightest hesitation, Lady Evelyn raised her stick and brought it down on his head. Checked in mid-step, his hands came up, his feet slipped on the polished floor. With a crash, he went down and lay unmoving, his eyes closed.

There was a long silence. Nobody moved—least of all the stranger.

"Naturally," said Lady Evelyn at last in a faint voice, "all I was trying to do was trip him up."

Anabelle looked at her. The old lady was breathing fast; her body was shaking. Anabelle took her gently by the arm.

"You're coming up to your room with me, and you're going to lie down for a little while," she said gently.

"I was only trying to . . . to trip him up."

"Yes, I know. You were wonderful," crooned Anabelle. "You tripped him up beautifully. He just banged his head a little, and as soon as I've seen you upstairs, I'll come down and see to him."

Lady Evelyn had no objections to raise. She went slowly up the stairs and consented to lie down—for a few minutes only, she said—on her bed.

Anabelle went to the window and opened it; Luis was coming towards the house.

"Luis," she called, "will you take Foguete home? Lady Evelyn is tired, and she's going to lie down for a little while."

"Can I come back—later?"

"Yes. Come back when Olivia has given you some tea."

She went to stand beside Lady Evelyn's bed.

"You won't try to get up?"

Lady Evelyn, her eyes closed, moved her head slowly from side to side.

"No. Promise me you'll . . . ring up the . . . police."

Anabelle hesitated only for a moment; then she realized that matters had gone too far for her.

"I promise," she said. She drew the curtains. "Can I get you anything?"

"No, thank you."

Sitting on the bed, she took one of the long, bony hands into her own, saying nothing, waiting until Lady Evelyn's breathing became more normal. She studied the soft, lined face and saw it as perhaps she had never seen it before. A proud face. A thin, obstinate mouth. Self-will written on every line. An arrogant, overbearing, rather stupid, certainly spoiled woman. A woman without tact; an interfering woman; all in all, a woman difficult to like. She herself, Anabelle understood in the cool, dark silence, had little or no liking for her. But she loved her.

She left her at last and went downstairs. She paused at the telephone, and then she went on to the drawing room; she could not, she felt, leave the man lying unattended.

She opened the door. The room was empty.

There was nobody outstretched on the floor. There was no sign of any stranger. It might have been a dream, a nightmare, an hallucination.

Might have been—but for the little round spot of blood on the floor where the stranger's head had rested.

She went upstairs; this time she did not pause at the telephone; it was one thing to call the police to report an intruder, but there seemed no point in bringing them to the house to look at a small round bloodstain.

Creeping into Lady Evelyn's room, she saw that she had fallen asleep. After looking into the kitchen to ask Mrs. Pollock not to disturb her, she went home. She walked slowly at first, and then she began to hurry, and at last she found that she was running—but she did not know why.

As she neared the house, she slowed her pace, but her heart was beating loudly and a sense of foreboding weighed on her heavily and made her reluctant to enter.

She went into the hall. Through a window she could see Foguete chasing imaginary rabbits in the woods. There were sounds in the kitchen and in her father's room—and then both doors opened simultaneously and she saw Olivia and her father.

"Where's Luis?" she asked.

Her father walked slowly downstairs, taking off his glasses as he came. Olivia had not moved.

"Where's Luis?"

Mr. Baird's voice was gentle.

"Luis has gone, my dear."

For some moments she could only stare at him. With a strong effort, she forced herself to speech.

"Gone? You—let him go?"

"I had to let him go. The man who was assaulted by Lady Evelyn—"

"I told you. He was on the train—and he didn't even know my name. He had no right—"

"He left the big house—escaped was the word he used—and met Angus at the gates. Angus stopped his car and spoke to him and found that you were with Lady Evelyn—but he guessed that you had found the brief case, and he guessed that it would be here. He came to fetch it—and I had to give it up; it contained papers sent by Luis's grandfather—the papers concerned Luis. Angus read them; he told me what they were, and after that I had no possible authority. . . ."

She spoke from a dry throat.

"Did Angus go with him?"

"The three went together: Angus, the man . . . and Luis."

"Where did they go?"

"For the moment, to London."

For the moment . . .

"Angus is coming back at once—that is, as soon as he has shown Mr. Sanders the papers. He is bringing Mr. Sanders back here. The man—the Portuguese—wanted to make a charge; he said that Lady Evelyn had attacked him."

"Is Luis coming back with Angus?"

"I don't know. Mr. Sanders is to examine the papers —but Angus said that there was no doubt that they were genuine."

She turned and without a word walked past Olivia and sat down at the kitchen table. The whole thing, she told herself in a desperate struggle between reason and emotion, the whole thing was over and could be filed as a strange incident in which she had played a brief but not unimportant part. She had been asked to look after Luis; she had looked after Luis. Now she was no longer required to look after Luis. The end. Now she could go on with life as it used to be before

Luis entered it. All she had to do was go on living—without Luis.

And without Angus.

She loved them both. They had taken Luis away; she had sent Angus away.

Life as it used to be. She had a pony . . . and a dog.

"Tea."

It was Olivia's voice. Anabelle had not known she was there, but she had come in and she had boiled a kettle and made tea. She sat on a stool opposite Anabelle and looked at her curiously.

"When you took it on," she said slowly, "you must have known that this was ahead of you."

"Yes, I suppose I did."

"It won't interest you too much, the way you're feeling now, but Clare and Keith are home. They rang up from London. They're on their way down now; they're going straight to the cottage to leave the boys—and then they're coming here. Are you listening?"

"Yes."

"I thought we might walk over and wait for them. Angus and Mr. Sanders can't be back before about six at the earliest. Will you come?"

"No. I think I'll stay here."

"Just as you like."

Olivia stood up.

"Luis left a message," she said.

Anabelle did not move.

"He wanted to wait until you came home, but Angus thought it would be better to . . . to go at once. Luis asked me to tell you that he would come back."

Anabelle said nothing. Olivia stood staring at her, seemed about to say something more, and then turned and went out, closing the door behind her.

Chapter Ten

At about seven o'clock, Mr. Sanders telephoned from the big house: would Anabelle and her father come over?

The summons—for such they understood it to be —was a relief to them both; for the past few hours, their own house had seemed like a morgue. Olivia had gone to the cottage to await the arrival of Keith and Clare; she had taken Foguete with her and had not returned.

On entering the drawing room of Steyne House, Anabelle looked first for Luis. He was not there. But there were others: the Portuguese stranger was present, a crossed strip of plaster on one side of his head. Mr. Sanders was there, small and pale and reedy-voiced, as Anabelle had always known him. And Angus was there, standing by one of the long windows; their eyes met, but he made no move.

From the shadows of the long curtains emerged Lady Evelyn, and beside her Anabelle saw Keith. She spoke to him as he came across the room to join her.

"Where's Clare?"

"She's with Luis."

"With . . . Where are they?"

"At the Coach House."

"They're not; I've just come from there."

"And they've just gone over there. No"—he

checked her as she began to speak—"I know it's all confusion, but that's why we're all here—to sort it out. Sit here."

She sat on a small sofa and her father came to sit beside her. Keith walked over and took his place beside Angus. Anabelle, looking round, thought that it looked like a committee meeting; Lady Evelyn must have thought so too, for she was sitting upright in her usual high-backed, tapestry-covered chair and addressing them in a chairwoman's manner.

"We're here," she said, "because Angus has insisted on our hearing Mr. Sanders. There is no possible question of assault. That gentleman over there"—she looked at a point above the Portuguese stranger's head —"entered my grounds and was loitering there without permission. I sent for him, and he happened to lose his footing on this highly polished floor. That is all."

"Quite so, quite so, Lady Evelyn," fluted Mr. Sanders. He was seated at a small round table, some papers neatly arranged before him. "But your grandson felt that it would be in everybody's interest to know why the Portuguese gentleman came here. And before I can explain this, I must begin by explaining something else: how it was that the little boy called Luis came to be at Steyne."

He paused and directed a mild glance round at everybody present; then his eyes rested on Lady Evelyn.

"I have your permission?"

She made a sign of assent. Mr. Sanders, with a dry preliminary cough, began his explanation.

"The boy," he said, "was brought up in Portugal by his grandparents, Senhor and Senhora Ribeiro. Early this year, Senhora Ribeiro died; and on her death, her husband found that some important papers relating to the boy's birth had been mislaid, or destroyed or—as he had reason to believe—hidden. The papers were, as I have said, important; they were all-important, for they were papers relating to the question of the boy's legitimacy. In other, plainer words" —Mr. Sanders, for all his reediness, made them very

plain indeed—"was the boy or was the boy not a bas-
tard?

"On the death of Senhora Ribeiro, a strong claim
for the boy was made by his uncle—brother of the
boy's deceased mother. The uncle wanted the boy to
live with him and to be brought up with his own children—but the boy, Luis, did not wish to go to his
uncle. His wish, of course, was to remain with his
grandfather—but Senhor Ribeiro was aware that he
had not long to live, and that any alternative arrangement he wished to make for the boy must be made
without delay. So it was decided that Luis should be
sent to England and kept there until the missing papers were found. The boy could not be sent openly,
for it was feared that the uncle would learn of the
plan and take the matter to the courts—but if he was
to be sent secretly, who would take him? Who could
be trusted to look after him, to give him care and attention and something which in his grandfather's view
was even more important: affection.

"The family priest, Father Vicento, solved the difficulty; he learned that a young English lady was
shortly to return to England on a Clarkson ship from
Leixoes. He made enquiries—and I do not have to tell
any of you how searching these enquiries can be
when conducted by a priest in a Catholic country. He
learned what he wished to know of the young lady's
background, and also of her love of and talent for
looking after children. To reassure Senhor Ribeiro, he
took him to a local fair which the young lady was to
visit, and here Senhor Ribeiro saw, spoke to, and
formed his own highly favourable opinion of the
young lady. Nothing then remained but to secure a
passage on the ship for the boy, see him safely aboard,
and pray earnestly that the young lady would play
her part by guarding the boy until he was claimed."

Mr. Sanders stopped, his eyes on Anabelle.

"I have here," he continued gently, "a letter which
I will give you presently. It is from Senhor Ribeiro; it
was written on the day before he died—written, in
fact, on the day after the missing papers were found.
For found they were. The boy's legitimacy was

proved beyond all question. The papers were not sent to England; they were brought, at Senhor Ribeiro's request, by this Portuguese gentleman, a distant cousin of the family."

Mr. Sanders paused to glance at his notes.

"We need not," he said, "go into the details of why or how the papers were, for a time, missing. Mr. Baird gave them to Mr. Angus Pemberton this afternoon, and I have examined them thoroughly. Knowing that the boy had won the affection of you all, I would have liked to have said that he might remain here—but this is impossible. He is at this moment at the Coach House with Clare—with Mrs. Trevor. She is packing his things. I came here to reassure this Portuguese gentleman that the . . . the attacks which were made upon him were made solely because of a mistaken idea that he had come to remove the boy illegally. I came also at Mr. Pemberton's request, because he felt that you would all like my assurance that nothing can stand in the way of the legitimate claim made upon the child. For the fact is"—Mr. Sanders glanced round the circle of attentive faces—"the fact is that the boy has been claimed by his father.

"The claim of a father is, of course, the strongest claim of all—and it was this fact that made the search for the papers so vital a one. Senhor Ribeiro had reason to believe that the papers had been hidden by his wife. During her lifetime he had felt unable to act, for to do so would have been to incriminate her and to disclose that on the death of her daughter—the boy Luis's mother, who died in giving him birth—she had been so determined to keep the child that she had concealed the fact of his birth from the father, and had registered the boy in Portugal under a name that was not his but hers: Ribeiro. It was impossible for her husband to betray her—but on her death he felt that the time had come to put the boy's father in full possession of the facts. But first he must prove that the boy was in fact the son, the legal, the legitimate son, of his father.

"This has now been proved. Nothing remains but to thank Miss Baird for her courage and devotion—and to let the boy go." He glanced across the room at Angus. "May I ask you," he said, "to go across to Mr. Baird's house to fetch the boy?"

Angus hesitated. He looked at Anabelle—and then his eyes rested for a moment on his grandmother. She was sitting as upright, as unmoving as she had done throughout Mr. Sanders's address—but her cheeks were paper-white, and the thin, blue-veined hands were gripped tightly together. She spoke without removing her gaze from the neat, impersonal papers on Mr. Sanders's improvised desk.

"Fetch him," she said quietly. "If he's got to go, he's got to go."

Without speaking, Angus walked to the door. The Portuguese rose, bowed stiffly to Lady Evelyn and to Anabelle, and then followed him. The sound of the car was heard for a moment and then died away.

"There is just one more thing." Mr. Sanders took out a snowy handkerchief and wiped his brow. "But before coming to it . . . I shall be glad to answer any questions."

He waited. Nobody had any questions to ask.

"Then," he proceeded, "we come to the question which nobody has asked but which is doubtless in everybody's mind: the question of whether the boy's father will be a suitable guardian for him. The answer is that he will be—but the history of the marriage must be briefly told.

"It was an unwise marriage; the couple loved one another, but they were not well suited. Even so, things might have gone well if from the first Senhora Ribeiro, the wife's mother, had not been so bitterly opposed to the marriage. She worked hard to part them, and before the year was out she succeeded. For a Catholic, there could be no divorce—but when the wife realized that she was to have a child, she decided that she would go back to her parents. She said nothing to her husband of her pregnancy. She bore the child at the home of Senhor and Senhora Ribeiro and, as I have said, died in childbirth, leaving the baby with its grandparents—and leaving the father ignorant of all the facts except one: that his wife was dead.

"The child's grandfather, Senhor Ribeiro, wished to inform the father of the child's birth, but his wife opposed him so bitterly that he was afraid she would not survive the death of her daughter and the parting with the baby to a man she so violently disliked. He promised that he would say nothing; he allowed his wife to register the child in their name—but he himself, looking into the future, determined that the truth should one day be known. He went to Oporto and there registered the child in its true name and its true parentage . . . at the British Consulate."

He stopped. A sound, low and inarticulate, had come from Lady Evelyn. He finished his story with his eyes on hers.

"For the father," he said, "was an Englishman. An Englishman who fell in love with a young Portuguese girl who had gone to Brazil to visit relations there. An Englishman who, at last learning of the existence of his son, came hurrying to Portugal to claim him, only to be checked by the fact that no papers were available. When he telephoned to me, I informed him that he could go to the British Consulate at Oporto and obtain copies of the documents, or a copy of the birth certificate—but to Senhor Ribeiro, finding the papers meant restoring, in some measure, the honour of his late wife. So the search went on—but while it was going on, the boy had to be sent away to prevent any move on the part of his uncle.

"I see that I do not have to tell you, Lady Evelyn, that Luis is in fact Luis Antonio Jose Pemberton, son of Angus Pemberton and his wife Laurinda, married six years ago in Brazil. Angus wished to bring his son home to you, present him to you—but he realized that it was one thing to bring over a child whose claims were legitimate; it was another to come to you with a boy he could not prove—although he himself had no hesitation in believing—to be his own. He had to wait—and he waited. Until today. I should like to say that from what I have seen of the boy, he is a great-grandson of whom you can be proud—but you will understand that the first claim, the strongest claim, one that nobody can challenge, is the father's.

Luis must go with his father. Luis has in fact"—Mr. Sanders, unable to go on looking at the immobile old lady, dropped his eyes to his papers—"he has in fact gone with his father. His father has taken him away and will not return for ten days. He will spend them showing the boy something of the land of which he is a citizen—England. When he returns on the twelfth of June—which, as you know, will be his thirtieth birthday—he has instructed me to say that he will either take up permanent residence in England or . . . he will return to Brazil."

Mr. Sanders rose, gathered his papers together, and then seemed to remember something.

"Return to Brazil, I should have said, with his son —Luis Pemberton."

Chapter Eleven

IT WAS EASY to trace the route. Highly coloured postcards arrived with unfailing regularity every morning—for Lady Evelyn and for Anabelle. They were addressed by Angus; the space usually filled in by Having A Wonderful Time bore only a forest of uneven crosses intended to represent kisses.

These communications, which gave Anabelle a soothing sense of nearness to the travelers, drove Lady Evelyn to a state of mind bordering on frenzy. It was a sheer waste of time to take a child to the Shakespeare country; she wanted particularly to be the first to take him to the zoo. Why the Pool of London? He had no interest in ships; his interests were purely military. Madness, letting an imaginative child visualize all those ghastly tragedies at the Tower of London, and pure sadism to let him see Mme. Tussaud's Chamber of Horrors. The New Forest was better; at least there were the ponies; Devon yes, unless he made the child ill with all that cream.

Since it was impossible for her to settle down to any kind of work, Anabelle kept her hours at the big house to a minimum and took refuge herself in a steady, relentless succession of domestic activities. She distempered the hall, turned her father out of his room on the pretext of repapering it, and when it was done fell to jamming and bottling.

But she learned, as she worked, all that Keith and

Clare could tell her. She learned of Angus's reluctance to use her as a shield for Luis; she heard of his wish to tell her the truth at the beginning, and his feeling that if he did so he would be involving her in a conspiracy of silence against Lady Evelyn.

"He had the most terrible trouble getting a passage on the *Yeoman*," Clare told her. "It was full. Then Keith heard that the Parker girls were traveling, and he knew that if there was a chance of getting a man on board who was less than a hundred and four, they'd manage it. And they did. I don't know who they threw off, but Angus got on. Even at the last moment there was some hitch about his ticket, and he nearly missed the ship."

"From the first," Keith said, "he was determined not to let you sail alone with Luis. He didn't know how you were going to react; if you panicked, he wanted to be there to steady you; if you didn't panic, he had four days in which to get to know Luis. When he got home, he told your father, and asked him not to give him away. They talked about money for Luis's keep, and your father said no; Angus said he'd arranged to have money sent from Oporto, and your father said it would do to buy a pony."

"But once the papers were found, why all the mystery about getting them here?" Anabelle asked.

"Old Senhor Ribeiro. Remember that he'd had this weight of guilt on his mind for years. After more than five years of soul-searching, after losing his wife and getting in touch with Angus and tearing up the floor boards to get at the missing papers, do you expect him to sit down and shove them into an envelope and post them? Haven't you ever heard of *l'amende honorable?* He sent his most trusted second or third cousin—and Father Vicento sent a telegram to say he was on his way. All the cousin was told to do was make his way to Steyne, go to Steyne House and put the papers—personally—into Angus's hands. And that's just what he was setting out to do when you met him on the train and sent him on to Yeovil and places west. He found his way back to London—a story in itself, if you ever want to hear it—and set off again next day, brief case under arm, and got as far as the house and was walking up to ring the front door bell in the normal way, when he caught sight of a small boy—a small foreign boy. He knew very little about the kind of papers he was carrying; all he knew was that they concerned a small Portuguese boy. All he wanted to do, when he hurried after Luis, was to hear his own language spoken. So he followed him—and you chased him up a tree."

"And then what?"

"After that, he went back to London and tried to get in touch with Angus by phone. But Angus, if you remember, was in London, and so wasn't available—and so he decided to come down to Steyne again, to look for his brief case. Which, as I told him, was an act of the highest courage; you should have seen how pleased he was when I—"

"Stick to the point," said Clare.

"Well, he came down and tried to find the tree up which he imagined his brief case to be reposing—and you know the rest."

"He admits that he lost his head," Clare said. "He admits that when the police were mentioned he panicked—and that's all he remembers until he sat up and fingered the lump on his head. He made for the station, but by what he called the intervention of Our Lady, coming into the gate as he reached it was a car —and in the car was Angus. After which his troubles were over."

"To come to Angus's troubles," Keith said, "how is Lady Evelyn?"

"We've been there twice, and each time she's felt too ill to see us," Clare said. "Is she ill?"

"No."

"Does she say anything about anything?"

"She saw Mr. Gravely yesterday."

"Did she sign anything?" Keith asked.

"I don't know. I don't even know whether he came down on his own or because she sent for him. All I know is that when he arrived I was told—very politely —to go home."

"Hasn't she mentioned Angus?" Keith asked.

"Only vaguely, when she reads the postcards. And once she said that in her opinion he had done me a great injury by giving Luis to me and then snatching him away again."

She spoke calmly. Keith, watching her, knew that she had come to terms with the situation; he would have been surprised to know that Olivia had done more than anybody to bring Anabelle to her present tranquil state of mind. From the small, the stagnant pool to the rough, tossing sea, there to learn to swim —or to founder. She had stated that she and Clare knew what they wanted; Anabelle also knew, at last, what she most desired.

When she went over to the big house that afternoon, she found Lady Evelyn, for the first time since the departure of Angus and Luis, in the shop. She spoke sharply as Anabelle appeared.

"My dear, we've been far too lazy of late; here's a whole long list of things to be seen to. What's that in your basket?"

"Apple jelly, lemon marmalade, and two cans of peas."

"All put up by yourself?"

"Yes."

"Thank you. You were very wise to take your mind off . . . other matters."

But for Anabelle, the time for avoiding the subject was past; the travelers were to return in a few days, and she had her own plans for their reception.

"You mean Luis? They'll be back on Thursday," she pointed out.

"How do you know?"

"Mr. Sanders said so. I heard him, and so did you. It's going to be Angus's thirtieth birthday, and he'll be back, as he said he would. And he'll go away again —unless you keep him here. You know that, of course."

"Know it? Of course I know it! Blackmail!"

"In a way."

"In a way? In a way! What has this whole scheme been, from start to finish, but blackmail? You heard Mr. Sanders stating quite clearly that if anybody wanted a copy of the birth certificate, all they had to do was go to the British Consulate—at which Luis had been registered—and ask for a copy; no more. So why all this poor sick old man, and little boy sent to England, and so on? To ensure that I would see Luis and become fond of him. All that nonsense about not being able to present a son who might not be his son —pah! *There*, I grant you, there *I* was greatly at fault. How could I have seen him without at once recognizing that head and the way he carried it; that proud little walk; that superb seat on a horse, the light in his eyes when he marched up and down that terrace? Quilling; pure, pure Quilling. It was there for all to see—but with my mind full of the other reason for Angus's homecoming, I didn't see. I failed to see. And now I'm expected to fall in with all his plans; and if I don't, he'll take the boy away. Blackmail! To use a little innocent boy to gain his own ends! To put pressure on me, to cook up a scheme merely in order to prevent me from signing—"

"You're quite wrong. Angus told Keith, and Keith told me that when Angus got the letter from Mr. Sanders, he tore it up. The letter wasn't a surprise; you were only doing what all his life Angus had feared you would do. It was only when he got Senhor Ribeiro's letter; it was only when he knew that he had a son who could inherit this house, who could grow up here, that he decided to come home and try to save Luis's inheritance."

"If that's all he wanted, he has succeeded. I saw Mr. Gravely and took his advice; I shall make my will in favour of Luis."

"If you do that," Anabelle told her, "you'll lose them both."

"In other words, Luis—as I've already said in other words—is a threat; all Angus wants—"

"Angus wants nothing more than his due. He wants to live here with his son—and with you. If I know Luis—and I do, better even than Angus does—I know that he won't be happy at Steyne House unless you're in it. You've nothing to lose; you've everything to gain. You can have a grandson who'll oppose you, and a great-grandson who'll be your ally. Luis loves you. If you want to keep him, you've got to give in."

"Never! To be bullied, to be coerced—"

"You wanted Angus to be a soldier—and he refused. Can't you see that this is a military maneuver? He fought you, he was beaten, he retreated and returned with reinforcements. In Luis, you've got your soldier—subject to his father's cooperation. You've no choice. You've got to give in."

"Never!"

"And giving in, why not give in with a flourish? Why prolong a war you've already lost? Angus will come back on the day he said he'd come back—his birthday. Most men can celebrate their coming-of-age at twenty-one; Angus has had to wait until he was thirty. So why not celebrate? This house has been far too quiet for far too long. Light it up. Take the Quilling trophies down from the hall and put back the stags' heads."

"*Never!*"

"Put the shop into the back rooms and put your own furniture back into the reception rooms. Put down the carpets again. Put up the brocade curtains. Turn Angus out of his old room and get it ready for Luis. Get the Home Helpers to send out a team to dust and polish. Put the chairs and the canopies back on the terrace. Get out the silver and the china and the crystal. Get out all Angus's old, forgotten, despised tin soldiers. Open up the playroom, get the rocking horse out and have its tail mended and—"

"Never!" declared Lady Evelyn passionately. "And besides, the tail is far too tattered. We shall have to have a new one."

Chapter Twelve

"It was, of course, your idea," Angus stated on Thursday evening.

"The whole thing," Anabelle said calmly. "But for me, you'd now be on your way to Brazil."

They were on the terrace, seated on long, cushioned chairs. Behind them, the rooms gleamed and shone. Dinner was laid for eight—a family party, with Mr. Sanders coming down from London to join them. Luis had seen no reason to be excluded but had agreed to compromise with a tea party in his father's honour. Now, after his bath, he had come down to say good night and was lying beside Anabelle on her chair, his arms round her.

"Who cooked the dinner?" Angus enquired lazily after a while.

"I did. Who else?"

"Plain or fancy?"

"Chilled soup, fish soufflé, steak—and Keith performing on the chafing dish. All right?"

"All right."

"Aren't you going to take Luis up to bed?"

"Certainly not. What's my grandmother for?"

"Bed," trumpeted Lady Evelyn behind them. "Luis, I am going up with you to see you settled."

"Be sure to hear his prayers," directed Angus, "and mind you don't get the denominations mixed up."

He got up, lifted Luis shoulder high, and swung him down again.

"Say good night."

Luis kissed him and then kissed Anabelle; with a yawn, he took Lady Evelyn's proffered hand and went indoors.

"We'll go in," Angus said. "It's getting chilly."

He put a light to the fire and he and Anabelle sat watching the wood blazing. There was silence in the quiet, dim room for a time.

"The only thing I can't figure out," Angus said at last, "is how you got my grandmother to take down those trophies."

"I'd given up," she confessed. "Then the secretary of the Outersteyne Institute came round for donations, and when I heard that they were appealing for decorations for the walls, it seemed like Providence. Perhaps it's an odd place for irregular cavalry to end up, but it all looks rather impressive. Your grandmother's going to open it formally at the end of the month."

He looked across at her.

"About Luis—didn't you ever have any suspicions?" he asked.

"Not until the moment that Mr. Sanders mentioned an English father."

"My grandmother will continue to accuse me, for the rest of her life, of having done you an injury—that is, in risking your getting fond of Luis. But you brought it on yourself."

"I did?"

"You told Ancell, that first time at the airport, that you liked small boys—all small boys. When I'd met Senhor Ribeiro and knew how matters stood, I remembered. It was that, I think, that took me to the Prendergasts'. I was in the room when Prendergast told you you'd got a berth on the *Yeoman*. The thing seemed to work itself out. The whole point, in my mind, was to make sure that I traveled home with you; I had to be with Luis . . . and I wanted to be with you."

There was a pause.

"What was she like?" Anabelle asked.

"Small and sweet—like you."

"Why didn't you tell your grandmother you were married?"

"I felt, at that time, that I'd cut myself off completely from her, and from Steyne, and from England. Later, of course, it became clear that I wasn't going to stay married long. She was in love with me, but she was the only child—and hopelessly and utterly unable to make a move without consulting her mother. I could see it wasn't easy for the parents; they'd gone on a short visit to Brazil, and they were appalled at the thought of going back to Portugal and leaving her behind—with a foreigner and a heretic. Her mother set out systematically to break it up—I quite honestly don't think she knew what she was doing; she loved her daughter, and she thought she'd be happier away from me. I thought she'd go back with them, but she didn't; things seemed to be working out, and I never understood why she did go finally. Now I know that she lost her courage—she couldn't face having the baby so far from what she still considered her home. And when she died, you can see why Senhora Ribeiro siezed the chance of keeping Luis and bringing him up as a good Catholic."

"Yes, I can see."

"And then I flew into Lisbon and looked down from the balcony and saw a girl playing with two small boys. I wondered whether my son would look like one of them. . . . And then I looked again and realized who you were. And then I watched you being drawn into the net—Luis, Father Vicento, Senhor Ribeiro, and the *Yeoman* and—"

He stopped, listened intently for a moment, and then went to the door and opened it. Without speaking, he beckoned to Anabelle, and she went quietly across to stand beside him.

On the far side of the hall, creeping cautiously, was Luis; his hand was grasping Foguete's collar; boy and dog could be said to be tiptoeing towards the stairs. They paused at the bottom; Luis looked to right and left, Foguete looked up and down; then they began a silent ascent.

Angus closed the door noiselessly.

"Aren't you going to do anything?" Anabelle asked.

He looked surprised.

"It's nothing to do with me; it's a problem for my grandmother. What he really needs, of course, is a stepmother. I'm seeing to it. I shall propose to you on your thirtieth birthday."

"You wouldn't rather have a younger woman?"

"Of course—but I know you like to think things over. If I rush you, you take fright."

"It seems a pity to waste all those years."

He turned towards her. At that moment the door opened and Lady Evelyn, resplendent in black lace and sequins, came in.

"Hush!" enjoined Angus, hand upheld.

"I haven't said a word; what do you mean by hush?" she asked.

"Anabelle is proposing to me; please let her finish."

"Anabelle is—" Lady Evelyn recovered and spoke decisively. "No. It would never do. You are not at all suited."

"That's what I thought," Angus said. "But if she insists—"

"My dear Anabelle, I have several nice young men in mind for you. If you had not got engaged to Philip Ancell, I . . ."

She stopped. There seemed no point in going on. Angus had taken Anabelle into his arms and was giving no sign of attending to her words.

"I love you," he said. "I love you with all my heart."

He was not addressing Lady Evelyn. She seated herself on a chair in front of the fire and spoke with resignation.

"Dinner," she said, "is at eight-thirty."